Pat Riordan returns...

...this time involved in a triple murder and the mysterious disappearance of a bank manager. Aided by his intrepid assistant, Reiko Masuda, who accepts an nonpaying job as "technical advisor" for some young men who run "mystery weekends", Riordan, in his usual clumsy fashion, is shot at and missed, swung at and hit by various suspicious characters.

Carmel is once again the scene of most of the action, and the search for clues covers the Monterey Peninsula, and all the way to Big Sur. The live oak? It's a wonderfully durable tree.

Live Oaks Also Die

Roy Gilligan

Live Oaks
Also
Die

BRENDAN
BOOKS
P. O. Box 710083
San Jose, CA 95171-0083

Brendan Books
San Jose, CA

Art Direction by Robin Gilligan
Photography by SplashStudios
Cover Art by Reed Farrington
Typography by Instant Type of Monterey

Copyright © 1990 by Roy Gilligan
Published by
  Brendan Books
  P.O. Box 710083
  San Jose, CA 95171-0083

Manufactured in the United States of America

  1 — 90

Library of Congress Catralog Card Number: 90-91654

ISBN: 0-9626136-0-6

For Brendan and Emma
May their lives be filled with the good things.

AUTHOR'S NOTE:

I T IS CUSTOMARY to declare that this book is a work of fiction, and that any similarity, etc., etc., etc.

It is quite true that this book *is* a work of fiction. The events described herein never really happened. The characters are all made up. *However*, the Carmel River Inn is a real motel, and a nice quiet place to stay. It has never, to my knowledge, been the scene of a murder. Most of the restaurants mentioned by name are real. Two of them I have neglected to identify: La Provence in the American Tin Cannery, and Beau Thai, on Cannery Row. La Provence is now Fish and Basil. Beau Thai (wonderful name) is still quite nice and doing well.

I want once more to thank my friend Reed Farrington for his striking artwork on the cover, and his portrait of me, which unlike that of Dorian Gray, remains the same, while its subject grows older. Reed was also gracious enough to lend his persona for the character of Greg Farrell. Thanks to Pat Mueller-Vollmer for the use of the house at Sixth and Santa Rita in Carmel, a city which, of course, is completely fictitious. And a proper Japanese bow to Cheryl Yemoto (nee Masuda), who not only posed for the character of Reiko, but lent me her maiden name.

Finally, my heartfelt thanks and deepest affection to my daughter, Robin, who put together the many complicated operations necessary to produce this book's cover, despite the gentle handicap of a 2-½-year-old son and a six-month-old daughter, my altogether exceptional grandchildren.

Live Oaks
Also
Die

1

I can be really important. Damn!

I̶T IS FAIRLY WELL KNOWN in theatrical circles that *Macbeth* is a bad luck play. In one documented nineteenth-century incident, the actor playing Macbeth used a real dagger to kill King Duncan and, indeed, dispatched the poor soul playing his majesty. During a London performance in the thirties, Olivier's sword snapped during a duel scene, sending the point rocketing out into the audience. The missile struck an astonished theatre-goer in the chest and brought on a fatal heart attack. At a later time, the gentle actress playing Lady Macbeth sleep-walked off a platform and fell twenty or thirty feet to the stage, fracturing a few unimportant bones but stopping the show cold.

I wasn't thinking of all those shows biz mishaps when Reiko came into my office to tell me that she had been invited to be a guest expert on a "mystery weekend."

"What the hell is a 'mystery weekend'?"

She was patient with me. She is not always patient.

"It is when a bunch of people stay in a hotel and solve a fake murder. It's a very popular thing."

I had been dimly aware of the "mystery weekend" or "mystery party", as practiced by bored society people who had grown tired of cocktail conversation. You paid your money—often an impressive amount, depending upon the accommodations, the meals, and the elaborateness of the production—and you played detective.

I remembered one in Monterey that featured a number of obsolescent "celebrities" (people from defunct TV series, movie stars you haven't heard about in years, Edd "Kookie" Byrnes) who, along with customers who had paid a grand apiece for the privilege, were lodged in a big new expensive (empty) Cannery Row hotel, and remained juiced or confused or both for the better part of three days. They had all come up on a sort of troop train from LA with a no-host bar.

"Why you, Reiko-san?"

A few tiny creases of annoyance appeared at the corners of her eyes. "My cousin Amy knows one of the men running the show. She had a couple of classes with him at Stanford. He asked her to help them because she knows the Monterey Peninsula, and she told them that I work in a real private investigator's office. It was, like, I could be a sort of technical advisor. You know, like in the movies. Am I going too fast for you?"

"No, honey, you're making yourself quite clear. When and where does this deal take place?"

"This weekend. At a neat Victorian-type hotel on Foam Street. Everybody checks in Friday afternoon and stays Friday and Saturday nights. It winds up Sunday morning. I'll have to leave early Friday— if it's all right."

She knew damn well it was "all right."

"It's OK."

Sure, little one, go along and play detective. I can see it now. Heavy melodrama, smoking guns. Knives dripping blood. Bodies all over the place. Clues scattered hither and thither all over the Peninsula. A giant game of "Clue." Back ten spaces. Do not pass GO.

"How much do you know about this murder party, Reiko-san?"

Her face brightened with excitement as she left the door frame and bounded into my office to perch on the side of my desk.

"Well, there's like twenty couples, and Cal and Bobby and Amy and me, and the actors..."

"Wait a minute. Cal and Bobby?"

"They're the guys who organize these things. Bobby's the one Amy knows. Remember?"

"Oh."

She plunged on, building up a head of steam. "Everybody checks in, and the guests and the actors are all mixed up. There's drinks and dinner and everybody mills around, and pretty soon one of the actors gets murdered, and...."

"Hold it." I signalled a time out. Reiko looked genuinely annoyed.

"You are behaving like a teenager. You have helped me through some real murder cases in the umpty years you've been with me. And in all that time, I have never seen you break your celestial calm. And now you're excited about a phony murder case staged for the entertainment of a bunch of people who can afford to spend many bucks to be amused on a November weekend that promises to be rainy. What's the big deal?

"Damn it, Riordan, it's just *because* I've been your stooge for umpty years! With this thing I get to be *technical advisor*. I can be really important. Damn!"

She was pretty mad. I had gone too far. I stood up, took her by the hand, and kissed her gently on the forehead.

Reiko and I had been together for nearly ten years, ever since she had walked into my grimy office in San Francisco, fresh out of school, looking for a job. She had signed on as a one woman office staff, more or less out of pity for me. God knows I couldn't pay her what she was worth. I was wrapped in a terrible long-term hangover when she found me, a widower wallowing in self-pity less than a year after Helen was killed.

I probably owe my life to this small *sansei*, barely five feet tall, with a face like an oriental doll. She took me over, organized me, got me going. She moved with me to Monterey a little while back. We had become more like partners than boss and secretary.

"Reiko, forgive me. You *are* really important. You are the most important person in the world to me. If it weren't for your stubborn old mama, I'd have married you long ago."

She brightened. She has a glorious smile and uses it often. The Japanese do not smile much, even third and fourth generation American Japanese. Often with them a smile is a sign of nervousness or embarrassment. There are traditional or genetic behavior traits that persist. But Reiko's smile is luminescent.

"It'll be fun, Riordan. It's a good script. I met the author the other night. He's an old guy from San Jose. He's got a beard. Looks like a cheap copy of Hemingway. The guy teaches school and writes detective novels on the side. Seems nice but very quiet . . . maybe a little weird."

"What's the story, technical advisor?"

"Well, there's a plot that involves a real estate swindle, and a subplot about a valuable painting, and a guy gets killed Friday night and his body is found in the hotel lobby, and the man's young wife is kidnapped, and another lady is killed the next day, and the final clue is at the lighthouse in Pacific Grove. . . ."

I placed my finger gently against her lips. The preposterous plan for this "mystery weekend" was a little too much for me. Two murders, a kidnapping and a board game delivered to the paying customers in a day and a half.

"Go thou, my dear, and advise. Have a good time."

"Then I can take off early Friday?"

"You bet, kiddo. You've got a freeby in a classy hotel, so enjoy. By the way, how much do the innocent bystanders have to pay?"

"Two hundred and fifty dollars. Apiece. Includes meals and two drinks. It's kind of a budget murder."

"Two fifty. Twenty couples. Ten thousand. Ought to be a few bucks profit in that. Hey, see if you can cut your old PI friend in on the next one."

Another bright smile. "They're rehearsing tonight. Well, it's really *discussing*. It'll be mostly improvisational. We're going to meet at the Grovemont Theatre in New Monterey." She hopped down off my desk and did a little dance toward the door. Just before she ducked out of my office, she paused, jerked her thumb toward her chest and said, "I'm the *technical advisor*." She winked broadly and disappeared.

Reiko had no notion of what she was getting herself into. It all seemed so innocent. A bunch of fun-loving people who like to read mystery stories get a chance to solve a make-believe crime. Just a lot of laughs, right? What could possibly happen? It's only playacting, it's only fake blood. But don't forget what I told you about *Macbeth*. Make-believe can sometimes get out of hand. When she popped out of my office Reiko didn't have a care in the world. She had never heard of Harry Levine. Or Olin Vanderhof. But she sure as hell would, very soon.

After she left, I went about my business, writing a long boring report for a Silicon Valley electronics firm. Although it's something like sixty-seventy miles to the northeast of my office on Alvarado Street in Monterey, Silicon Valley is a rich source of my business. It's not all that exciting, but it pays the bills. On the day that Reiko told me about her big job as a technical advisor, I was winding up a security check for a widget manufacturer. Thank God I don't have to know what the widgets do, I just have to check up on the people who work there.

When I finished my snitch report it was around seven and Reiko had long gone. I locked up and left the office to walk down Alvarado to a Chinese restaurant. I count myself a sort of gourmet when it comes to Chinese cuisine. Not the hot stuff, the Szechuan and the Hunan. That's for people who don't really want to taste anything. Cantonese, that's the stuff with the delicate flavors.

I sat, sipping tea and contemplating the long menu. If I had been in San Francisco, I might have expected a couple of black-clad gunmen from some sort of Fu Manchu outfit to come in and spray the place with Uzis. But there were only six people in the place, including me and a party of five blue-haired old ladies and, besides, nobody shoots up a place in Monterey. Nobody gets gunned down in Monterey. But then, I hadn't ever heard of Harry Levine, either.

2

"Banks operate on a delicate balance."

N EXT MORNING— it was Thursday — I was sitting in my office nursing a cup of very strong black coffee from the bakery downstairs, and staring out at the traffic in Alvarado Street. Nothing of any consequence was going on. The late autumn rains had begun and the street was wet. Thanksgiving was a couple of weeks away. The few people on the street looked glum. Young urban professional Californians do not approve of rain.

Reiko was working out a final draft of my employee report for that what's-its-name company on her IBM-PC. She always swears in a small voice while engaged in word-processing, and her vocabulary is shockingly scatological. But she gives the naughty words a ladylike music.

I heard footsteps in the outer office. Then the sound of a gentle male voice: "Pardon me, miss, is Mr. Riordan in?"

"Goddam!" said Reiko. "You nearly scared the livin'...." She caught herself just in time.

I couldn't see her from where I sat, but I got the picture. Startled from her concentration, she had hit a wrong key and wiped out half a sentence. But, being Reiko, she recovered quickly, and in a singularly graceful motion, rose from her Norwegian knee-chair and smiled her brightest smile.

"Who shall I say is calling?" That sexy gelato voice can captivate any male within earshot.

"My name is Vanderhof, Olin Vanderhof. Mr. Riordan doesn't know me. I am a . . . business associate of George Spelvin of Pebble Beach."

"Send in the gentleman, Reiko." Since the whole conversation took place within ten feet of where I sat, I saw no reason to go through any formalities. Besides, George Spelvin (not his real name) had been my benefactor. Any friend of George had to be a friend of mine.

Olin Vanderhof was tall and thin, a good six inches taller than I am. He had a hawk-like face with high cheek bones and deep creases from eye to jowl. His eyes were dark and shining, and he had a thick head of silver gray hair. He wore the kind of cast iron suit that you expect to find on undertakers and old high school principals.

We exchanged the usual forgettable opening phrases, and I gestured toward my only guest chair.

Vanderhof never took his eyes off me. He didn't look at the chair, he didn't glance out the window. He sat down slowly, and his long lean frame seemed to fold like a road map.

A faint smile broke the vertical lines of his face.

"Mr. Riordan, George told me that you are completely trustworthy. The matter I wish to discuss with you requires absolute confidentiality. May I count on that?"

"Mr. Vanderhof, I have no wife, I do not talk in my sleep . . . when I do not sleep alone. The only person in the world who must share some knowledge of my cases is the little lady in the other room, and she, despite her delicate beauty and her weakness for profanity, is a veritable rock."

He seemed to relax. "I am chairman and principal stockholder of a small bank in San Benito County. We've been in business only half a dozen years, but we've done rather well. There's great wealth in San Benito, you know."

I had heard that many times. San Benito County is a place of mystery to most Californians, and totally unknown to the rest of the world, even though U.S. 101 runs through a corner of it. Hollister is the county's only town of any size, and the only thing that Hollister is noted for is an invasion of motorcyclists in the late forties that was preserved for posterity in a Marlon Brando movie.

Better known but much smaller than Hollister is San Juan Bautista, a colorful Hispanic California village made somewhat famous by Alfred Hitchcock in his late fifties movie, "Vertigo." Who can forget Jimmy Stewart struggling with his acrophobia while Kim Novak dives from the Mission belfry.

Vanderhof was examining my face for...what? Signs of interest? Of honesty? He continued:

"I started the bank. I got together a group of investors—George Spelvin is one of them—and we applied for a charter. It was to be a sort of home town operation, specializing in personal service to the San Benito farmers and ranchers. We thought we could take some business away from the big boys of San Francisco. And we were right.

"However, none of us knew much about banking. So we had to hire somebody who did to set up and manage the bank—a man with experience. And we thought we had found one in Stewart Leonard. Stewart came from Pittsburgh or Cincinnati or one of those places back there. My family has been in California for six generations, so I'm a little hazy about those eastern cities. Leonard came to us through an executive placement agency and was highly recommended. And he served the bank well...it seemed...until just last week when, ah, he, ah, disappeared."

The man seemed to be straining to believe what he had just said.

"I don't think you mean, Mr. Vanderhof, that he was sitting at his desk and vanished in a puff of smoke. The guy ran off with a lot of money, right?"

My visitor coughed a deep, rattling cough and whisked from his breast pocket a white linen handkerchief which he pressed to his thin lips.

"No, Mr. Riordan. So far as we know, nothing is missing...except Stewart Leonard. My own accounting firm—men I have known for many years—is examining the books, but so far they've discovered no shortage, no problems. Do you mind if I smoke? I know it'll probably kill me, but I can't break the habit."

I nodded. Vanderhof extracted a silver cigarette case from an inside pocket and removed a cork-tipped cigarette. My God, I thought, how long has it been since I've seen a cigarette case?

He replaced the case and produced a gold Dunhill lighter of ancient vintage and lit his cigarette with an unsteady hand.

"Stewart is unmarried. Or so we were informed when we hired him. He was only thirty-five or so when he came to us, and he had risen quite rapidly to vice president and branch manager of a large bank in Cincinnati . . . or Pittsburgh. We were impressed by his youth and enthusiasm, and by his obvious grasp of banking affairs. When we gave him the job, he chose to live in a condominium near the junction of Highway One and the Carmel Valley Road. It meant a fairly long commute, but Stewart said he preferred the cool climate and green foliage of the coast to the heat and dryness of the inland valleys."

There was a prolonged silence and Vanderhof stared—for a change—at the top of my desk.

"Banks operate on a delicate balance." He grimaced. "That's a rather bad unintended pun. But it's true. The least bit of doubt or suspicion and . . . you're out of business. We've managed to cloak the absence of Leonard with a hastily confected tale of a family emergency in the East. None of the employees is aware of the true circumstances. But the fact is, Mr. Riordan, that Stewart had no family in the East that we can locate. And he hasn't been in his condo since a week ago Monday. We want you to find him for us. Or, failing that, to find out what has happened to him."

Vanderhof filled his pauses with long drags from his cigarette which he blew straight up into the air, contaminating the small space of my office, and fouling my sinuses.

I considered my options. Young, single bank executive disappears. Wait, he must be fortyish. Is that young? I remember when I was . . . what the hell, never mind. No embezzlement. Vanderhof's own accountants examining the books. The guy is probably in Cabo San Lucas with a new beard and a twenty-year-old girl. Unless he's gay.

"Ok, Mr. Vanderhof, here's the deal. I'll give you two weeks. If I can't find anything in that time, you'll owe me two thousand dollars plus expenses. If I *do* find the guy—even if it's in two *days*—you'll owe me *five* thousand plus expenses. How does that strike you?"

"Fair enough, Mr. Riordan. George says you're good—and

honest. That's enough for me."

We stood up and shook hands. After he left my office, I found that in the absence of an ashtray, he had allowed his cigarette to burn out on the edge of my desk. That, goddammit, was the first item on "expenses."

3

If it's alive, it's not dead, right?

GEORGE WAS ON THE PHONE the next morning.

"What do you think of Vanderhof, Pat? Bit of a stuffed shirt, eh?"

"I don't know, George. He seemed pretty straightforward to me. How long have you known him?"

"A hell of a long time. We were at Santa Clara together. I thought the sonofabitch would go for the priesthood. The Jesuits were really working on him."

"What has he been doing, George? Besides the banking thing."

George waxed nostalgic.

"Married a girl he met when he was in college. She was homely then and she's homely now . . . but she's one of the best people God ever made. Gave him four smart kids, and is a helluva cook. They've got a place up on Loma Alta Road. Plenty of money from both families. Olin's like me. Never had to work. Why I let him con me into that bank deal, I just don't know. I dumped all my big bank stocks, Pat, in that October mess, remember? Who'da thought they'd go sour?"

I was satisfied. George was sober. And he had stayed sober (and, surprisingly, married) since his current wife was convicted (on a plea bargain) of manslaughter in the murder of one of her women friends in what the immortal Inspector Clouseau has called a "rit of fealous jage." I shouldn't make light of what happened to Debbie Spelvin, though. She's still, in many ways, *The Woman* to me. But that's another story. George, who is in his latish sixties, is a real sweetheart

13

by nature, but unpredictable when drunk. And drunk used to be his natural state.

He went on: "I never got directly involved in the bank, Pat. Just wrote him a check. I still can't understand why they hired that nigra to run it. What do those people know about money?"

So Stewart Leonard is black, I thought. Why didn't Vanderhof tell me that? Why did George say "nigra" like my old Virginia grandmother used to?

"Don't know if I can tell you any more, Patrick. Keep me posted. Find the guy. There's a pretty good chunk of my capital at risk. Bye-bye."

He hung up, leaving me with the receiver pressed to my ear for five or six seconds before I could react to his abrupt departure.

I called out to Reiko: "What's that guy Vanderhof's number? You got it out there?"

She came to the door, looking smug, waving a piece of paper. "His office is over on Calle Principal. Here's the phone number. You remember I'm leaving early today, don't you? For the mystery week-end thing."

"Oh, yeah. How's that going?"

Her eyes lit up and she started her little dance. Reiko has this odd and endearing little way of showing excitement. She bounces around on her toes when she talks, staying within a two-foot square, and her hands fly about her face like golden butteflies.

"It's going to be great, Riordan. They're such wonderful actors. And the director is just fabulous. The script's fine, but the author just sat in a corner and looked worried. I don't think the man ever laughs."

"Hooray for homicide, honey. Leave when you must, and have a good time. Hey, where's the dinner going to be? I might want to drop in and observe from the sidelines."

"It's at that French place in the American Tin Cannery. We're supposed to be there at seven." She giggled. "There's going to be a kidnapping!"

"Look for me, Reiko-san. I'll be the lonely fellow in the false mustache at the corner table."

She bounced back into her antechamber with a shrill, musical laugh, a sharp contrast to her usual throaty Japanese growl.

There's going to be a kidnapping. Maybe there already has been a kidnapping. Or a murder. Anything is possible. Bank manager held for ransom. Bank manager murdered for the combination to the safe. It could figure. I punched out Vanderhof's number.

A man's voice at the other end: "Vanderhof Trust."

"Mr. Vanderhof?"

"I'm sorry, this is his secretary speaking. May I say who is calling?"

"Riordan. He'll know."

The hold went on. Mantovani. Something lush and romantic with about two hundred violins.

Vanderhof came on: "Mr. Riordan, have you located Leonard already?"

"No, sir. Haven't really begun to look. Need some information. George Spelvin tells me that Stewart Leonard is black. Did you deliberately withhold that information—or was it just an oversight?"

A moment of silence.

"By all means an oversight, Mr. Riordan. One doesn't even consider those things these days, does one?"

He wasn't convincing.

"Are there any other black persons employed by the bank, Mr. Vanderhof?"

"No. As a matter of fact, we had just about decided to hire Stewart because of his excellent references before we met him. He's a man of great dignity and charm, not like...."

He stopped cold. It's still there with this man, I thought. The old "credit to his race" bit. But I guess those ideas fade slowly (or never) with a lot of people of Vanderhof's generation. And maybe some of my own generation.

"Thanks, Mr. Vanderhof. I think now I have a better idea of the man I'm looking for."

I spent the afternoon going over the personnel file on Stewart Leonard that I hadn't got around to looking at since Vanderhof dropped it at my office. Parents deceased. No siblings. Nothing about race. I guess they don't put that on these things any more.

B.A. and M.B.A., University of Cincinnati, *summa*, no less. Trainee with Third Union Trust Bank, Cincinnati. Steady progress to VP, Walnut Hills Branch. References include city councilman, several clergymen, and one Taft.

It was pretty dark when I left the office. Except for the rain and an occasional violent storm from the Pacific, the weather is pretty much the same the year around on the Peninsula. It never gets really freezing cold, as it does in the inland valleys of California. There are always flowers in bloom, and most of the trees are evergreen. Aside from the pines and cypresses, there's the live oak. That name puzzled me for a long while. Seems so self-cancelling. If it's alive, it's not dead, right? But, I guess, live oaks also die.

I get depressed sometimes on November evenings. Ordinarily, I'm a reasonably happy guy in my solitary life. I'm not all *that* lonely. I have a few well-chosen friends who invite me over for dinner now and then. I have Reiko who, although she has several prosperous suitors panting after her, I suspect will never marry. And in recent months, I've had Sally Morse.

Sally's a travel agent I met last spring when I was contemplating some sort of trip. I wanted to go somewhere—just *go* somewhere. When I asked George for help, he put me in touch with Sally. She's a tall, slender woman with some gray streaks in her dark red hair that were not produced in a beauty parlor, and a hell of a sense of humor. After a couple of consultations, a couple of lunches, and a couple of dinners, we wound up spending a week on Maui together. Only then did I get up the courage to ask her if she was related to the prominent Morse family of Pebble Beach and the Del Monte Forest.

"Hell, no, Riordan. My ex-husband is a trumpet player. He does studio gigs in LA. Do you think I would be wasting my time with you if I had connections with money? Well, I guess I would." With that, she rolled over and went to sleep.

On this particularly gloomy November night, however, Sally was not around. She was in Paris as a guest of the French Tourism Bureau, checking out the new delights and more expensive tourist traps of the City of Light. God, how I envied her.

I went out to the restaurant at the American Tin Cannery to watch the "mystery weekend" get into action.

It wasn't difficult to identify the participants. They were a solid group on one side of the dining room. The actors were not hard to pick out. They looked sober and nervous. Reiko and her cousin Amy hovered, bright-eyed, on the outside edge of the group. Two young men I took to be Cal and Bobby conferred earnestly with the maitre d'.

If you are wondering what kind of people come to this sort of shindig, imagine a high school basketball game in Minnesota. Or a social gathering at a national political convention.

Some of the men wore ties, some didn't. One or two wore suits, a few more wore sports jackets, the rest sweaters or leather jackets with knit cuffs. Some looked dazed, and others were loud.

The women were uniformly self-conscious. Half of them were dressed for competition, or at least a cocktail party for Dan Quayle. The other half were content with slacks and blouses, although it was evident, as always, that the women with the biggest asses wore the tightest pants. Several ladies had fur jackets hanging carelessly on their shoulders.

I looked 'em over at my leisure. At the center of things sat a beefy man of fifty wearing a diamond pinky ring of such magnitude that it flashed reflections all over the dining room when he signalled the waiter. Next to him was an exotic, dark-skinned woman who seemed aloof, but smiled cooly at her dinner partner's obtuseness.

At the same table was a couple who seemed to have got into the wrong group. They sat stiff and silent, watching the others with tight smiles.

Everybody (with the obvious exception of the displaced pair) was having fun. They had had enough to drink to loosen them up, and they were bantering loudly with each other as if it were a class reunion. They all wore name badges the size of three-by-five cards. Occasionally one would visit another's table and there would be a great fumbling for glasses for hyeropic middle-aged eyes to read the nicknames on the tags.

I discovered through unhappy experience long ago that booze makes you feel smart and talk dumb. And there was an awful lot of talk in that room.

I nursed my Perrier and fresh lime. I used to be a professional drinker, but I lost my title. I hadn't been to this place before, and I seemed to be the only man in the place with neither jacket nor tie. A waiter with a long nose was regarding me with suspicion. Time dragged on. Cal and Bobby were trying desperately to get their people to eat. I had some sort of duck dish that was very good, but my waiter seemed all too eager to snatch up my plate and run me out. I think he sized me up as a bad tipper by the rumpled sweater, jeans and running shoes.

After an hour or so, when the mystery weekenders had eaten and the food had taken the edge off the booze, somebody must have given the signal for action. A large man with artificial gray at the temples stormed into the place and confronted a pretty young woman and her escort, people I had pegged for actors when I first saw them. There was a loud argument. From what I could hear, the large man was the young woman's husband (in the play, of course), and she was being discovered in a romantic tryst—God, I love euphemisms for lustful attachments—and the husband was threatening both of them with mayhem or worse. The big older man pushed the boyfriend in the chest, and he went down hard, taking the tablecloth with him. Out of the corner of my eye I saw the maitre d' wince and cover his face.

The paying guests were all riveted now, most of them standing to get a better look. The younger man sat on the floor, dazedly wiping chocolate mousse from his expensively coiffed hair. The young woman was sobbing in an unconvincing manner. The enraged husband stalked out of the restaurant, pausing a second at the door to project a baleful gaze at the entire group.

I started to applaud, but thought better of it. Weekenders began to buzz and the buzz got louder by the second. The young couple managed to stay in character, and in a short while the whole bunch got up and moved toward the door. Completely enchanted, I followed them.

Outside the restaurant, everybody just sort of stood around. Reiko sidled up to me and pinched my arm, rather viciously, I thought. Suddenly, a black limousine drove up. Two serious-looking actors leaped out, grabbed the young actress who had figured in the recent confrontation, and flung her (gently, with tender loving care) into the car. They drove away, trying, I'm sure, to burn a little rubber, but not succeeding.

The young leading man (or juvenile, as we theatrical people say) dashed madly, hopelessly after the car, and disappeared around the corner.

Only then did I notice the mild-looking, bearded fellow standing in the shadows, worriedly taking notes. The author. A thankless task, his. Writing books must be tough enough. Writing for the stage may be a little worse. But writing for a bunch of party animals who surround the action has got to be difficult indeed. The author wandered off into the dark. The crowd dispersed to look for more excitement. They were about to find a hell of a lot more than they expected.

I drove back to Carmel and went to bed.

4

"There wasn't even much blood. Just a hole. . . ."

ON SATURDAY MORNING I awoke about seven, shaved and showered, and drove down to the Crossroads for breakfast. Early morning is the best time of day in Carmel. Weekends are touristy even in November, but on Saturday morning the tourists are sleeping in, and the parking lots are virtually empty. You can even find a place to park on Ocean Avenue, the broad central street of the town, a string of T-shirt shops that runs from Highway One to the Pacific.

The Crossroads, a sort of satellite cluster of shops and restaurants, is near the junction of Rio Road and Highway One, not far from the condo complex where I had been told Stewart Leonard lived. I had decided to take a preliminary look around and, besides, there's a little breakfast place used mainly by locals that won't strain your bank account. My artist friend Greg Farrell and I meet there at least once a week to exchange war stories and other lies. He did a couple of turns in Viet Nam, I went reluctantly to Korea. We talk art, too. I try to keep up with what he's doing, and he asks politely about my dog pictures. He knows I don't (read "can't") paint any other subjects but dogs, happy or sad, slick or fuzzy.

On this Saturday, however, I wasn't meeting Greg and art was not on my mind. I finished breakfast and drove down to the dead end of Rio Road. It was no trick to find Leonard's condo. Vanderhof had somehow employed a discreet locksmith who had opened the door and made some new keys, one of which had been left under the mat for me.

I let myself in. The furniture in the living room was relatively new and, I guess, in excellent taste. The decor was white and off-white, chic as hell, and straight out of *Architectural Digest*. This was a bachelor's pad? It was as if the most expensive decorator in Carmel had done the place, and then nobody ever sat on anything.

Beyond the living room was a small dining area and a spotless kitchen, also apparently untouched by human hands.

Up a short staircase was the single bedroom. There was a king-size bed, neatly made, a chest of drawers, a closet full of clothes, and occupying a corner of the room, an elaborate computer layout, complete with modem and printer, recognizable (even to me, a computer idiot) as one of the most advanced and expensive on the market.

I switched on the machine and waited. Nothing. The monitor was blank. I tried poking several keys at random without result. I gave up. This was a job for my friend, the technical advisor. Reiko could make any computer lie down, roll over, and retrieve sticks.

After inspecting the neatly arranged, expensive suits and jackets in the closet, and rummaging through the drawers in the chest, predictably finding nothing, I went downstairs, peeked into the closets and kitchen cabinets, carefully locked the door, got into my maltreated Mercedes two-seater, and headed for Monterey.

Surprisingly, the door to my office was slightly ajar when I approached from the drafty flight of stairs that lead up from Alvarado Street. I'm not the nervous type, but I confess I got this little squirt of adrenalin as I neared the door. *Nobody* on my floor comes in on Saturday morning. *I* certainly don't usually, but hell, with Sally out of town, and Greg holed up in his studio consumed with a new project, and my utter contempt for golf, where else should I be? I wanted to study the file on Stewart Leonard further, to look for something I had missed, to get some kind of lead after striking out in his sterile apartment.

One of those other guys would have slipped his thirty-eight out of a shoulder holster, kicked the door all the way open, and, assuming that spread-legged, two-handed pistol stance, yelled "Freeze!"

I pushed the door open with the back of my hand and looked at Reiko, sitting on her heels in the Japanese fashion on the tatami mat I had stolen for her. She raised her head slowly and turned toward me. Her eyes were frightened.

"A man got murdered last night, Riordan. At the hotel. They found him in his room, dead, shot between the eyes. I saw him, Riordan. There wasn't even much blood. Just a hole...."

"Well, hell, Reiko-san, wasn't that what was supposed to happen? Wasn't that what the deal was all about? How did the paying customers react? Is the game afoot?"

She shook her head slowly.

"You don't understand, Pat. This wasn't part of the act. The wrong man got killed. One of the guests. The actor who was supposed to get killed just took one look and got sick all over the floor. The other guests all tried to get the hell out, but the Monterey cops were there in a hurry, and got all the names and addresses. Cal and Bobby were just devastated. I had Amy drop me here on her way home...."

I sat down on the mat beside her and put her head on my shoulder.

"Things got a little more technical than they should have, honey. Must have been pretty traumatic. Here, come on. Let's go downstairs and have a cup of coffee. Maybe it'll help. And I want to hear the whole story."

5

"Nobody saw her leave."

W E SAT FOR AN HOUR in the bakery downstairs, drinking coffee. It is a good indication of the seriousness of Reiko's shock that she drank coffee at all. She hates the stuff. I ordered a piece of Danish for her which she ignored.

Her voice was strangely muted as she told me the story: "After dinner—you know, when the fellows kidnapped the girl—the group kind of broke up. That was the way it was supposed to be. About eleven o'clock everybody was supposed to meet back at the hotel, and the body of Rhett Carstairs was supposed to be found in the lobby with a knife in his chest."

"Rhett Carstairs?"

"Yes, the older man who came into the restaurant during dessert and pushed Lance Steinbeck around."

"Lance *Steinbeck?*"

"The young hunk with the shellacked hair who was romancing Celeste Carstairs...."

"Wait a minute, wait a minute. We're getting into the realm of romance novels. Pretty soon we'll be talking about alabaster breasts and sinewy forearms. Who really got killed?"

"A man named Harry Levine from San Francisco. I don't know anything about him. Except that the lady he was with was *not* his wife, even though he introduced her as his 'Hawaiian bride', and he was what you call a venture capitalist, and he had a big house in

Pacific Heights, and he owned a lot of property in Carmel Valley, and...."

"Stop! A real mystery man, eh? Where'd you get all that information?"

"Well, they had a cocktail party at the hotel, and everybody was drinking and I...just...sort of...*listen*."

"People lie at cocktail parties, Reiko-san. I bear the scars of many cocktail parties, and I know how much people lie. Can any of this stuff be checked out?"

"The police might know something. Cal and Bobby had the man's home address, but nothing else."

"Well, we'll see, dear. Maybe I ought to take you home. Did you get any sleep at all last night?"

"None, Riordan. Amy and I went up to the Dream Theatre after dinner to see a picture with Billy Crystal, and when we got back to the hotel, everybody was supposed to find Carstairs' body in the lobby with the knife. But somebody noticed Levine wasn't there. Cal went up to his room on the second floor to check, and in a couple of minutes came back yelling. Then we all went up to Levine's room, and there was this hole in his head...."

She put her hands over her eyes in the "see no evil" position, and rocked back and forth.

"Where was the guy's, uh, female companion all this time?"

She looked at me. "She was gone, Pat. Her bag was gone. None of her things were in the closet or the bureau. Nobody saw her leave."

"Anybody know her name?"

Reiko shot me a sidelong glance. "She was registered as 'Mrs. Levine', dummy. You know how those things are. Even her baggage fitted the character. The initials were "S. L." I heard Mr. Levine call her Sylvia."

I gave Reiko a little hug. "It's your case, honey. You're the technical advisor."

"I'm so disappointed. I mean, it's awful, the man getting killed and all. I was so looking forward to the game. I've seen all the clues and figured out all but one. It was just a slip of paper that read, 'Behind the soap man's castle on the saddest street in Carmel!'"

"Well, that is probably damn clever, and I've no doubt you'll solve the problem, but right now, I think you need some rest."

I went around behind her chair and helped her up. Her solid little body was dead weight. She leaned against me on the way to the car, and fell asleep during the ride out to her apartment in Pacific Grove. I had to carry her up a steep flight of stairs, and I understood clearly indeed what John Gielgud said about playing *King Lear*: "Get a *light* Cordelia."

6

"What the hell, bank's a bank."

At the corner of First Avenue and Torres Street in Carmel there is a standard street sign bearing the familiar legend, "Not A Through Street", to which a local philosopher had added in a black scrawl, "nor an easy life." If there is one eternal verity that I have affirmed, it is the truth of that sign. Unfortunately, some uptight soul during the Eastwood regime saw fit to clean off the impromptu inscription. A shame, a dirty shame.

On a day-to-day basis, I have no great problems. When I lost my wife suddenly in an accident on the highway, I was nearly destroyed. I suffered terribly, and even though many years have passed, I still get a stabbing sensation in my gut when I think of that night . . . and that loss.

But things have gone reasonably well for me since. The work I do is routine and most of it is not fun at all. But every once in a while something really interesting pops up. The disappearance of Stewart Leonard was one of those somethings.

Clean-living bank executive one day does not show up for work. He has left no word, his condo is empty (and spotless). He has no family. Nothing appears to be missing (yet) from the bank. No reason to suspect foul play. But the fact remains that the man is gone.

It was about ten o'clock that Saturday morning when I left Reiko safely tucked in at her apartment and drove up Forest Avenue in

Pacific Grove to the Holman Highway and over to the Highway One interchange. I took the north loop in the direction of Santa Cruz. It was an overcast day, even a little nippy, but dry so far, and as good a time as any to take a leisurely look around in San Benito County, and maybe get some inspiration.

North out of Monterey you go through sprawling old Fort Ord, famous through three wars as the Infantry basic training center for the West Coast. On the ocean side of the road, against the dunes, are the firing ranges that trained many a foot soldier to shoot acceptable scores on targets, but never quite got 'em used to the idea of shooting people.

As the road nears Castroville ("The Artichoke Capital of the World"), State Route 156 veers off to the east and connects with U.S. 101, the westernmost of the great highways running from Mexico to Canada, and known intermittently as "El Camino Real." Some of the glamour (but not much of the traffic) is gone, now that Interstate 5 plows through open territory in six- and eight-lane glory. But the royal road is still the royal road.

I headed north toward San Francisco, and in a short while, turned east again on the continuation of 156 that runs through San Juan Bautista to Hollister. With the earliest fall rains, the hills were beginning to green up a bit after the parched summer. There are two ways to interpret California's self-established title as "The Golden State." People generally hook up the name with the Gold Rush of the mid-nineteenth century. But when the stranger finally arrives here on his summer vacation, he's often surprised to see mile after mile of golden hills that haven't seen any water since March, dotted with dark green scrub, looking pretty desolate. One of my old army buddies used to like to refer to California as the "world's second largest desert." A shade exaggerated but true, I guess, to a degree. Without the elaborate irrigation system and the dams that trap water from the winter rains and the mountain snow, we'd be a kind of temperate zone Saudi Arabia.

It's mostly hot and dry in the summer in San Benito County. Occasionally a little fog sneaks over the hills and provides a bit of moisture. But in late November, the hills were looking pretty good.

The first place you hit on Route 156 in San Benito County is San

Juan Bautista. It has one of Father Serra's Missions, the one from "Vertigo", remember? But when you see it you think, hell, Kim Novak might have survived that dive from the bell tower, unless she landed on her head. San Juan is also painfully rustic. Tobacco spitting contests on the bench in front of the general store and all that. But it is, in its small way, another tourist trap. Some decent Mexican restaurants, a carefully preserved main street, and an antique shop that has what might be the most extensive collection of Havilland china in North America.

But what fascinates me most about San Juan is that it sits right smack on the San Andreas Fault, that notorious meeting of land plates that promises, sooner or later, to separate California into two long, skinny states. When I was young and idealistic, I wrote a poem that began, "Lemming-like I fly / To stand astride the San Andreas Fault / And dare the earth to open up and take me." Pretty morbid, huh?

There's a new four-lane divided highway from 101 that bypasses San Juan, but soon thereafter it narrows into a simple country road that goes the nine miles further into Hollister, a town I can best describe as "western isolated", an island in time. I hadn't been there for years and I wasn't prepared for the signs of decay I saw along San Benito Street, the town's main drag. San Juan is old, picturesque; creaky, but preserved. Hollister is nondescript; a town that strongly resembles the settlements that are strung along the central valley of California from Sacramento to Fresno. It is the county seat of a farm county. Whereas San Juan has a mission teetering on the edge of the San Andreas Fault, Hollister has the Masonic Temple at Fourth and San Benito, with an elaborate clock tower, and a thousand pigeons. Hollister also has a Chinese restaurant that advertises that it serves breakfast. I had a milkshake at a handy McDonald's.

Outwardly, with the exception of a certain amount of apparent decline and some boarded up shops, downtown Hollister hadn't changed much over the years. I parked the car and walked down San Benito Street, peering into store windows as I went. On a whim, I opened the door of an unpainted store front which bore the sign, "Sam Pearcy, Insurance."

A very large man wearing a cowboy hat and a multi-colored

flannel shirt was sitting at the only desk in the place with his lizard boots resting on a top drawer and his nose buried in the financial pages of the San Francisco Chronicle. He didn't seem to hear me come in.

"Mr. Pearcy?"

The paper was lowered very slowly. Under the Stetson was a great, fleshy red face with a large nose on which was resting a wire-rimmed pair of half-glasses. The man gave me a thorough examination before he spoke.

"I'm Sam Pearcy. If you come about insurance, you're outa luck. Don't sell insurance no more. Just keep this place so I can get away from my wife. Sorry, pardner,"

Somehow I'd expected him to call me "pardner."

"No, Mr. Pearcy. I'm not in the market for insurance. I'm new in town and just askin' around. Tryin' to get some good advice from some of the old timers. Now, about bankin'. You got any recommendations on which bank treats you the best?"

I had fallen into a Texas accent of my own, the old Randolph Scott influence, and the more I talked, the thicker it got.

Pearcy laid down his paper and waved his arms. "Oh, any of 'em's all right. What the hell, bank's a bank. Wells Fargo's just down the way here. Good as any."

"How about the Farmers' and Ranchers'? I hear they take care of you real well."

His face clouded. "Not real sure about them guys. Only been around a four–five years or so. I know 'em all out there. Got a nigra fella runs it. Don't know's I'd...well, mister, you got to suit yourself."

"You know a fella named Vanderhof?"

"Ol' Olin, from Monterey? Hell yes. Good enough fella. I've knowed Barry Heathcote longer. He's one of the board members. Reckon I've knowed ol' Barry mebbe ten-twelve years. But that bank....? Mister, like I said, you got to suit yourself."

I thanked Mr. Pearcy and walked back to the car. The name Heathcote hadn't rung any bells. I headed out of town on Fourth Street, eager to get back to State Route 156 which would take me back to Monterey. Just before I hit the city limits, I noticed a cinder block building, a perfectly flat, one-story rectangle, bearing a sign that read, "Farmers' and Ranchers' Bank of San Benito County." Naturally, on Saturday afternoon it was closed.

It occurred to me that I might have a hand in keeping it closed permanently.

Maybe Stewart Leonard was just visiting his sick grandmother. On the other hand, maybe he was living it up at the Georges Cinq in Paris. or he might be floating in Monterey Bay. Whatever, I came out of Hollister with one new name and enough gas in the Mercedes to get me back to Carmel. And very little else.

7

"Hawaiian? Ha, c'est merde."

I AM ABOUT TO RECONSTRUCT (with a little poetic license) a series of events that Reiko described to me some time after they occurred. The quotes might not be the exact words, you understand, but what the hell. I'll bet you I'm damn close.

Reiko awoke about four in the afternoon after a fitful sleep during which she roused every fifteen minutes. Her first thought was to get out and do something about the murder of Harry Levine. I don't know what she thought she could do. But I learned long ago not to underestimate her.

I had tucked her in bed in a little nightshirt I found in a drawer. Despite my occasional twinges of lust, I had undressed her and put her down like you do a child who has fallen asleep in front of the TV. What a wimp, I thought. If the guys in the saloons I used to frequent could have seen me peeling the clothes off this perfect little body and pulling her nightie over her head without laying a hand on her, I'd have lost my macho card. But, as Cronkite used to say, that's the way it was.

Next morning (as her report to me began) she got up and showered, thought of the events of the night before (before she conked out, that is) racing through her head.

Reiko's first impulse in any problem situation is to run right at it full tilt. This technique can be very effective, but also occasionally destructive. I've admired this characteristic in her, but it has worried me, too. In the case of the "mystery weekend" which featured a real murder, she was determined to 1) take action, 2) leave no stone unturned, 3) plunge ahead and ferret out the evildoer, 4) all of the above. But she was likely to get her small neck stuck out too far.

She pulled on a sweater and jeans, emptied the cat box into the john, and put out a snack for El Gato, a large, bony tabby cat that permitted her to share the apartment with him. She called Amy, whose phone-answering machine provided one of those familiar fictions that precede, "When you hear the tone. . . ." Considering the threatening weather, she selected a shapeless hat from Banana Republic and jammed it down over her ears.

Frustrated, she walked down the stairs from the apartment, and out onto Lighthouse Avenue. The overcast was heavy and the street was damp, but no rain was falling. She walked briskly down through the business section of Pacific Grove, eyes straight ahead, ignoring the shop windows that would have attracted her on a normal day.

She turned west at Ford's department store to catch Central which mysteriously becomes Lighthouse again at the Monterey city line, a fact that has confused many a tourist over the years.

Cannery Row wasn't that far, and the day was meant for walking. When your mind is occupied, you don't notice distances. Reiko tugged her hat down against a rising wind.

Where should she start? she thought. Where would Riordan start? Well, *he* isn't always right. Take it as it comes. She looked up and found herself in front of the French restaurant at the American Tin Cannery, the place where it all began.

Where was Levine after dinner? The "wife", the "Hawaiian bride" was with him at the table. Who else was near? Was the woman outside during the fake kidnapping? Where did all the people go? Why the hell didn't I pay more attention?

She tried the door of the restaurant.

A man in shirt sleeves and an open collar appeared in the window and gestured at a "Closed" sign.

"We do not serve until six o'clock, madame. Six o'clock. Sorry."

Reiko put on her most authoritative voice. "It's about last night.

The private party. *You know.*"

The man's expression changed from a mild hauteur to a grim concern. He unlocked the door and let Reiko in.

"Are you with the police, little lady?"

"I am a private investigator, ah, in the employ of the people who organized the party." It was only a small lie.

The man sighed. "I have talked to the police today. There is nothing I can tell you. Those people. They were here, they ate, they left. They broke some china and glassware. What else?"

"Sir..."

"I am Marco, little lady, just Marco."

"Marco, do you remember the man who was killed?"

"There were so many. But—if I do not mistake, if I understand what the officers told me—it was the big man with the red face who sat with the very beautiful dark-skinned lady. He ordered a very expensive wine—which, of course, he had to pay for separately. The young men had arranged for house wine only, the Ernest and Julio."

"Marco, you have probably been in this business a long time. You notice things. You...*evaluate* people. All maitre d's do. What was your impression of Levine—the big man with the red face?

Marco pursed his lips and touched a nicely manicured index finger to his chin. He looked to be in his fifties, a shade under six feet, bald in a neat, classic way with no strands of hair trying vainly to cover the smooth, glossy scalp. He wore a clipped mustache under an admirable Roman nose. His English was accented only slightly.

"He is—*was*—I think you would say, a phony. The wine he ordered was expensive," a smile tugged at the corners of his mouth, "but not very good, *n'est-ce pas?* He was the kind of fellow who would order the costliest things on the menu and declare them to be good even if they were third-rate. No doubt he had money. But I suspect he had passed most of his life without it. An obscene tipper. He left a twenty-dollar bill, even though the gratuity was figured into the overall cost to the young men who had organized the affair.

"The woman with him was another matter. A striking beauty— with lots of class. Probably the most beautiful black woman I have ever seen."

Reiko was stunned for a moment.

"But he said she was Hawaiian."

"I'm sorry, my friend. As you say, I tend to. . .*evaluate* people. She had no hint of island or oriental blood. She was a gorgeous black woman. Hawaiian? Ha, *c'est merde*."

Reiko thanked the maitre d' and walked out into the gloom of a cloudy, threatening day. She walked up across David Avenue, past the Monterey Bay Aquarium a block down the hill to the left, and on a few blocks to the hotel which had been the scene of the murder.

At the desk she wanted to ask for Cal or Bobby, but for a moment she couldn't remember their last names. The clerk understood, however, and told her they were still in their room.

Bobby answered when she tapped at the door, looking rumpled, baggy-eyed, and a little drunk.

"Come on in, fortune cookie. Join the wake."

8

...*there has always been a suggestion of the Marine drill sergeant about Reiko*....

BOBBY LLOYD AND CAL WOODWARD are very bright men who are classic examples of the young and upwardly restless. They are single, ambitious and clever. Although they have probably never discussed the matter, each aspires to become CEO of a large corporation with at least a six-figure income. Now, however, both are in their latter twenties and employed in entry management positions with different companies, Bobby in San Francisco, Cal in LA. They have been running these mystery weekend things for a year or so, mainly by remote control, acquiring staggering phone bills, and piling up miles of air travel. Up to now, they've barely broken even. The Monterey event was to have been the bail-out, a sure fire profit-maker.

Bobby Lloyd is tall and thin with dark curly hair and pale skin. He has a perpetually worried look and dark circles under his eyes. Cal Woodward is about five-nine and round-faced. He has a ruddy complexion, blue eyes and an easy grin, even in moments of anxiety. He lay sprawled on one of the twin beds as Bobby led Reiko into the room.

She stood silent for a moment, batting away the smoke and liquor fumes with her butterfly hands. Bobby threw himself down on the unoccupied bed. Reiko felt a surge of quick anger.

"You delicate bastards! Get off your asses and on your feet and let's do something about this mess!"

Despite her fragile look, there has always been a suggestion of the Marine drill sergeant about Reiko as long as I have known her. She is not your shy, compliant oriental female, walking several paces behind her man, eyes cast down in deep respect. She is proud of her ancestry, but feels, in all honesty, that those traditional Japanese women were a bunch of wimps.

Bobby and Cal came to a sort of fuzzy attention, each assuming a rag-doll sitting position, reasonably alert, but ready to collapse with the slightest excuse.

"You guys have the list of people who paid to come on this fiasco. I know they're going to want some of their money back, if not all of it. I want to know where they are. Any of 'em still here?"

Cal rose painfully to his feet and walked unsteadily to a coffee table across the room. He pulled two pages stapled together from a sloppy pile of notes, receipts and cocktail napkins.

"Here, lotus blossom, take it away and let us suffer. We are out a lot of money. We do not give a shit about what happens because we are out of the mystery party business, too."

"Not yet, you aren't. You've got to go over this list with me and tell me all you know. I'm the *technical advisor*, goddammit!"

I really believe that at this point she thought she had a moral obligation to find out who killed Harry Levine. She had signed on with these two yuppish types as "technical advisor" at zero pay. She was well aware that the state of our offices finances was just a shade above chaotic, but she was about to throw herself headlong into a murder case for which we could not realize a thin dime.

Reiko knelt by the coffee table and sat on her heels. The two men reluctantly sat on the floor on either side of her. She brushed everything off the table with a wave of her arm and laid the list of paying guests on it, carefully smoothing out the wrinkles and scraping away a blot of dried cheese with a delicate pink fingernail.

"Now, who the hell are they?" she demanded, snapping her head from left to right.

It didn't take long to narrow down the list of twenty couples. Out immediately went the murdered man. His companion was already

numero uno on the suspect list. Out in quick order went others who
were 1) referred to the boys by family and friends, 2) their business
associates, and 3) potential clients of each with impeccable
credentials.

Only five couples had joined the party presumably as the result of
ads in the San Francisco *Chronicle* and the San Jose *Mercury-News*:
Levine and his blushing bride, Marsha and Eugene Fowler of Mill
Valley, Irene and Stanley Kessler of San Francisco, Anne and Carl
Shepherd of Sunnyvale, and—a late addition—Arlene and Joe
Caravelli, also of San Francisco.

"Something wrong with those ads," Bobby said glumly. "Never
pulled. Cost an arm and a leg. Shoulda used TV, maybe."

Reiko was busy copying down names, addresses and phone
numbers.

"Any of 'em still in the hotel?"

She hung the question in mid-air for either man to answer.

Cal responded first: "All gone out of here. I don't know whether
they went straight home or over to Carmel, or wherever else for
that matter. After the cops got through with 'em and we told 'em
they'd get most of their money back, they just split—into the
ever-lovin' goddam wind."

The two young men simultaneously lit cigarettes and Reiko made
for the door, anxious for fresh air.

"I'll be in touch, you guys."

And she left without looking back.

9

"Call girl? No such thing, detective.
You're an escort or you're a whore."

IT WAS COOL AND DRIZZLING as I turned down Sixth Avenue off
Carpenter in Carmel. My place (which actually belongs to George
Spelvin) is at Sixth and Santa Rita, near enough to town to walk, far
enough up the hill to be quiet.

As I approached and prepared to swing left into the driveway, I
noticed a light gray sedan parked in front of the house on the Santa
Rita side. It was some kind of Japanese car—they're all beginning to
look alike to me—or maybe one of those late model Mercedeses that
look like Japanese cars.

I parked and walked up the hill and around the corner. As I
approached the gray car, the door on the driver's side opened and a
woman stepped out and faced me.

"Mr. Riordan? I'm Shirley Leonard."

"Mrs. Leonard?"

"Miss Leonard. I'm Stewart's sister."

"Miss Leonard, how the hell did you get to me?"

She hesitated. "Can't we go inside? This is really pretty complicated and damned important. Besides, it's wet out here."

She was right. In addition to the drizzle, the water was dripping
from the live oak leaves, and we were both getting noticeably damp.

Shirley Leonard followed me down the stone steps to the two-
story Hansel-and-Gretel cottage I live in. In the dusk and the

overcast I hadn't yet got a good look at her.

I opened the door and switched on the light. If this house has a flaw, it's a lack of illumination in the living room. I took a quick look at Shirley and saw immediately that she was a strikingly beautiful woman, perfect features, and skin the color of light milk chocolate. She was wearing a lilac raincoat with a hood. I led her into the kitchen where I could help her with her coat—and there was better light.

I hung up the hooded coat on a peg near the back door. When I turned around, Shirley Leonard was sitting at the table in my dining alcove, her hands palms down on the table, waiting for me. I draped my wet jacket on the back of the chair and sat down.

In the brighter light, she was even more beautiful than I had thought. Her skin was flawless, her black eyes widely spaced and deep.

"You're thinking I'm a good-lookin' black broad, aren't you, Riordan? Ever since I was fifteen men have been looking at me just the way you're looking at me. Well, I've taken advantage of that look. It's made me a pretty good living. I'm a professional girl, Riordan, very expensive, highly recommended. But I'm not here on business. You're not my type, anyhow. That Mercedes of yours needs body work, and I know you don't pay any rent for this house. You're not in same league with *my* customers."

Sally Morse had told me once that I had a "certain naive charm." I resented that a little. I'd never thought of myself as naive. After all, I'm over fifty—some, a combat infantry veteran, a widower, and a licensed private investigator with nearly thirty years of experience. What the hell? Naive? That was bad enough. Now this Leonard woman tells me I'm out of her league—or out of her customers' league.

I tried to be cool.

"You're a call girl, then?"

She threw back her head and laughed until tears came into her eyes.

"I manage an *escort service*, Riordan. In San Francisco. Mostly I pass out assignments. Now and then I take one myself. It's a high class operation. Best in town. Call girl? No such thing, detective.

You're an escort or you're a whore. If you're a whore, you're on the street. If you've got class, you're an escort."

Maybe I *am* a little naive. Or maybe it's that it has never occurred to me to patronize professional ladies. There's always been somebody. I have never been much for one-night stands, let alone one-hour encounters.

"Let's get down to business, Miss Leonard," I said, flushing a little at my own unintentional double entendre.

"Call me Shirley."

"Shirley. You're Stewart Leonard's sister. You say. Why should I believe you?"

"Because goddammit, I *told* you. Listen, Riordan, I got no reason to lie to you. I've told you what I am. I could have said I was an Egyptian princess and you'da probably believed me."

"OK, Shirley. You came to me about Stewart. How come?"

She closed her eyes for a moment.

"Oh, shit, Riordan, I was down here on a job. I knew Stew was here, working at the bank over in that cow town. When I got to Monterey Friday afternoon, I called him. Stew and I haven't been close over the years. He didn't like my business. We never had a row about it. He just sort of cut me off.

"Well, they told me at the bank that Stew had gone back East on account of a family problem. Hell, I'm the only family he's got, and I'm *here*. When I made it sound kind of urgent, they told me to get in touch with a guy named Vanderhof in Monterey.

"I called Vanderhof's office and left a message. Last night I came back to my hotel with Harry—my, uh, date—and there was a note to call Vanderhof. I laid it on the line with him and he gave me the whole story, including all about *you*, and how you got this little freeby house from George something-or-other. That's one of my talents, Riordan. Gettin' fellows to talk. Anyway, he told me to get hold of you.

"I made the call on the lobby phone. When I got up to the room, good old Harry was crapped out on the bed, snoring. I figured I'd just skip this one. Harry was an asshole, anyhow. Big bullshit artist with too much money. I packed and got a cab over to the Plaza. This morning I rented a car and started snooping around. There was nobody at your office when I found it. So I just sort of drove around until this evening. Hey, this is a pretty funky little town. Somebody told me Clint Eastwood is the mayor here. That right?"

I had sat fascinated through this long tale. Not just because this woman was incredibly sexy and beautiful, but also because certain relays were operating in my head and flashing signals.

"Not any more. He still lives here, but don't start looking for him. It's a waste of time. About your date. Harry?"

"Harry Levine. Big operator from the City."

Harry Levine. Now late of The City. With a small caliber bullet hole between his eyes.

10

"You got money, it don't matter a damn.
You still get dead."

ONCE AGAIN, I am in the position of having to recreate Reiko's report as I got it from her. You must remember that she talks very rapidly when she's excited which is a good deal of the time. But I'm used to her chatter and feel justified in guaranteeing all the basic facts.

Reiko had a little list: The Fowlers, the Kesslers, the Shepherds, and the Caravellis. And, of course, Levine and his mystery lady. At this point, she didn't know what I knew about Shirley Leonard.

She knew a little about Levine, if what she had heard at the cocktail party had any truth in it. He came from San Francisco. He owned a house in Pacific Heights, where property is staggeringly expensive. He said he had a lot of land in Carmel Valley. He might have been lying. Make that he was *probably* lying.

Reiko has an efficient network of relatives throughout the eleven western mainland states and Hawaii. Her Uncle Shiro is our landlord at the office. He also runs a gardening service that covers the Peninsula. He is well connected.

She walked back to her apartment clutching her little list of names and addresses, frowning in intense concentration. By the time she got home, she had a plan of action. But she was totally exhausted and, besides, who can get anything done on a Saturday night? She had a glass of wine and a salami sandwich, and fell into a deep sleep with El Gato on the pillow beside her. She woke up, surprised to find that it was ten o'clock on Sunday morning.

The day had dawned bright and clear, in sharp contrast to the showery overcast of Friday and Saturday. Reiko bounced out of bed, made a cup of tea, and called her uncle.

"Hiya, kid, what's cookin'?" Shiro, who was born in Japan and speaks English with a heavy accent, loves American slang, but is always a couple of beats behind.

"Do you know anything about a man named Levine who owns a lot of property in Carmel Valley?"

"Reiko-san, that's like asking me if I know a man named Levine who runs a kosher deli on Fairfax Avenue in LA. Lemme see . . . Levine, Levine. Such a name. What's the front part again?"

"I didn't say. It's Harry."

"Oi veh, honey, you should have said that. Not that it helps a lot. Not the most unusual name in the world. But I have heard of a Harry Levine who's supposed to own some property in the Valley. He is also somewhat connected with what is called an investment outfit in San Francisco. And I remember something about a little bank in Hollister. Otherwise, I know nothing about him."

"He's dead, Uncle. Murdered in a Monterey hotel."

"It happens, chickie. You got money, it don't matter a damn. You still get dead. What's it to you?"

Reiko explained to her uncle her connection with the murder of Levine. He did not seem terribly impressed by the mystery weekend idea.

"Sounds like a con to me. Why would everybody want to be a detective. Oi veh! Anyhow, you can easily tell who perpetrated the crime. The broad! She whipped out her little roscoe and put one dead center."

"Thanks, Uncle. I'll keep you posted, and I'll call you if I need you."

She put her finger down on the disconnect button and immediately phoned me at home.

Before Shirley Leonard had left me the night before, she had told me all she knew about Harry Levine. She had had no contact with the man before the Monterey trip. He had been directed to her by another regular client whose name, she had told me gravely, she could not divulge. There is a certain code of honor observed by members of the escort profession.

"Stick around a little while, Shirley. At this moment I've got no notion of where your brother is, but I'm beginning to warm up to this enterprise."

"Sure, Riordan. I got nowhere to go. Maybe I can even open a branch office here. I been lookin' at the phone book in the hotel. You've got all kinds of travelin' masseuses here. Must be a great town for conventions.'

I escorted the lady to her car and sent her on her way. It's not that I would have objected to putting her up for the night. it was that crack about my not being in her class that turned me off.

Anyway, I had a pretty good night's sleep when Reiko's call woke me.

"What the hell are you doing in bed, Riordan. It's after ten-thirty."

"I was reading a book last night," I lied, "and it had me so absorbed I couldn't put it down." Actually, I had been watching a stupefying, sophomoric Saturday night variety show on TV until about one o'clock. I do that sometimes; watch a TV show that is abominably performed and written by cretins, so fascinated am I by the sheer stupidity of the thing that I can't turn it off.

"I've got news for you, Pat. Uncle Shiro has heard of Harry Levine, and you know what? He is tied up to that bank over in Hollister that the man disappeared from."

"I'm not at all surprised that Shiro knows who Harry Levine is. Shiro knows who *everybody* is. But I've got even more startling news for you, Reiko-san. The beautiful dark lady you told me was with Levine at the mystery party showed up here. She is the disappeared guy's sister."

"Shit, Riordan. One of these days I'm going to dig up something you can't match. Or maybe I'll quit and go to beauty college. or run a flower shop."

"Cut it out, honey. Your information is really more important than mine. Come on over here, if you've got nothing better to do, and we'll get a waffle at the Bistro.

11

"OK, Riordan, let's get down to business."

CARMEL-BY-THE-SEA, the village that I love, did not change a hell of a lot during the term of the invisible mayor. Oh, I guess, he wasn't *that* invisible, even though in the early months of his term you had to get a ticket for a council meeting. For although he had lived around these parts for a number of years, Clint Eastwood, mayor or not, was still a movie star.

Early one evening I was driving north on Carmelo Street, coming from a friend's house, and when I made the turn up Ninth Avenue, there he was, a tall, skinny, scowling figure, walking alone down the hill, clutching a sheaf of papers. His hair was cut short, and he wore a brown jacket, tan pants and a dress shirt with a necktie. If it hadn't been for the scowl, I'd never have recognized him.

I admire the man in a way. I've never been what you might call a fan. It's very difficult for me to see shooting people as a sport, even if they are bad guys. I know it's the American Way to idolize ol' Duke Wayne and even, I regret to say, Sylvester Stallone. I've got this deep-rooted resentment of guys who win movie wars against enemy troops or cattle rustlers, for that matter, but who've never had to dodge bullets for real. Stallone out there in his glistening bare torso, firing a machine gun from the hip, tends to make me retch.

But I'm inclined to think the real Eastwood is more like the gentler characters he's played: a quiet prospector who sang badly and shared a wife with Lee Marvin; the proprietor of a seedy wild west show; a tubercular folk singer; a soft-voiced, sexy disc jockey; a deputy from the West, out of place in New York.

But maybe the man's a complete bastard. Like another movie star who was blacklisted by the rental agencies on the Peninsula because he took an expensive house during the Crosby golf tournament and clogged the plumbing trying to flush down the Polaroid negatives from home-made porno pictures.

What got me thinking about Clint as Reiko and I walked down from my house (at a forty-five degree angle) to town, was the relatively new presence of the public johns in Devendorf Park at the top of the business section of Ocean Avenue.

Prior to the accession of Clint to the throne, Carmel was run by a succession of amateur politicians who apparently thought they could run tourists out of town by bursting their bladders. They fought for years over public restrooms. Paradoxically, they argued for—believe it—a quarter of a century over an expansion of the public library. The library now has the council's blessing.

And it really doesn't appear as if there are going to be any skyscrapers.

Why did the movie star run for mayor? He's an amateur politician, too. His pictures make good money. He has business interests nobody even knows about. He didn't need the two hundred bucks a month.

I think he just loves the place, like I do. And he was in a position to do something about Carmel.

Anyway, Reiko and I came down the hill to get a late waffle at the Bistro. It's a neat little place, plastered with local art, a lot of it the work of Greg Farrell's former students. My late wife, Helen, used to have a few paintings in here. My dogs never made it, although a particularly well-made Doberman was under consideration.

We munched thoughtfully in a corner. Nearby, absorbed in a Sunday newspaper spread all over a table, was a man well known for his sometimes humorous TV show in which subjects were secretly photographed doing embarrassing things. He's not nearly as recognizable now as he once was.

"OK, Riordan, let's get down to business." Reiko patted her lips with a paper napkin. It occurred to me that I'd never seen her use lipstick. For that matter, I can't recall ever seeing her apply any kind of make-up, at her desk or any other place. That's supposed to be a secretarial privilege, isn't it?

I cleared my throat like the chairman of the board. "Let's compare notes. There are quite a few interlocking pieces in what originally seemed to be two different puzzles. I've got Stew Leonard's sister, who was Harry Levine's date. Leonard is missing, Harry is dead. Harry might have been—at least if your uncle is right—connected with the Farmers' and Ranchers' Bank of San Benito County. Vanderhof will have to confirm that. A colorful character in Hollister dropped the name of Barry Heathcote. Says he's a member of the board. Leonard's sister has been on the outs with her brother for years and, if I can believe *her*, hasn't the faintest idea where he is. What do you know that's new?"

As I talked, Reiko seemed to be ticking off points in her mind. She thought for a moment.

"I went through the list of guests at the mystery weekend with Bobby and Cal. We were able to pretty well eliminate all but four couples. The rest were people either known to one or the other of the two guys, or otherwise vouched for by business associates. Of those left, one couple was from Marin, one from Sunnyvale, two were from San Francisco. I haven't had a chance to check on any of them yet."

"Marin County, that's Trendyville, U.S.A. Sunnyvale is Silicon Valley. You only get known in San Francisco if you go to the Washington Square Bar and Grill. Very good, honorable technical advisor. So what do we do now?"

She was very cool. She took a sip of coffee, wrinkling her nose in distaste.

"Tea's better. Well," she said, assuming the chairmanship, "you should talk with Olin Vanderhof, Riordan. I think he knows more than he's telling. I am going to track down those other people. Now, since we have to walk up that damn hill, let's get going."

12

"Sally Stanford was a madam.
Sally Morse is a travel agent."

I HAD NO LUCK reaching Olin Vanderhof Sunday. His home phone didn't answer, a thing I found curious in view of the fact that I was sure he had some sort of household staff. I figured that I'd have to wait until Monday to pay the man a call.

Reiko went back to her Pacific Grove apartment, bent on tracking down the four unaccounted-for couples from the mystery weekend. She proposed making a sweep of the Peninsula hotels and motels, on the theory that none of the couples could have gone very far. If that project proved fruitless, she'd call the home phone numbers she had gotten from Cal and Bobby. I could not convince her that it might be easier to do it the other way around. Call 'em at home first.

"They wouldn't go right home, Riordan. The weather's too nice."

You can't argue with that.

I had given her the name of a police lieutenant who might help her. I am not all that well acquainted with the Monterey Police. There just hasn't been much contact. I used to get into small personal altercations in bars during that black interim between my wife's death and the arrival of Reiko. But never in Monterey. I can't seem to think of any reason for that. Maybe Monterey has just become sedate since the days of Steinbeck and Doc Ricketts.

It was a beautiful day in late November, warm, not a cloud in the sky. I went out on the deck to enjoy the sunshine and had just stretched out in a canvas chair when the phone rang.

Muttering terrible curses translated from the Arabic, I pulled myself up, went into the house and grabbed the phone.

"Hello, goddammit," I said politely.

"Riordan, you're your old sweet self. I'm glad. I was afraid that during my absence you might have become nasty and difficult, or, on the other hand, turned gay on me. Come and rescue me from this miserable little airport."

It was Sally Morse, a couple of days earlier than I had expected her, and I couldn't have been happier.

"They call her Frivolous Sal, a peculiar sort of a gal," I sang in several different keys, "a wild sort of devil, but dead on the level was my gal Sal."

"Bullshit, Riordan. Come and get me."

I made it to the airport in about fifteen minutes. Sally was sitting at the curb on a Vuitton case, chin in hand, glaring at me, after the manner of Rodin.

God, she is a handsome woman, I thought, as Sally rose to greet me. But she's madder than a wet hen about something—or *everything*.

I kissed her and got very little response. She grabbed two large cases and moved to the rear of the car, waiting for me to open the trunk. Not a word of greeting. Not even a "gladtoseeya."

She glared at me as I lifted the deck lid and fitted in the cases.

"I have been in this godforsaken place for nearly three hours, Riordan. There's one limo in operation, and it left ten minutes before my plane landed. I've called every cab company in the phone book and nobody could promise anything. Then I started calling you, and your phone didn't answer and *didn't* answer. Where the hell were you on a Sunday morning? And don't try to tell me you were running on the beach, you bastard."

I helped Sally into the Mercedes and walked around to the driver's side. She was still fuming about the whimsical attitude of Air France, and the assholes who run airports, and the perils of modern transportation in general. She swore that she would give up the travel business for something like schoolteaching or aerobics instruction. As we pulled out of the airport and headed into Monterey, she slumped down in her seat, grew silent and remained so for the rest of the trip.

Last spring when I told George Spelvin I was pooped and disenchanted, he said, "Go see Sally Morse."

"I don't need a madam, George, I need a change."

"Sally is not a madam, you jerk. Sally *Stanford* was a madam. Sally Morse is a travel agent."

"What do I want with a travel agent? I know how to buy airline tickets and make hotel reservations."

"Trust me, Patrick. Sally knows all the angles. She's...she's more of a *therapist* than a travel agent. She analyzes you and then *prescribes*. Call Sally."

I didn't really buy all of what George was saying, but I decided to go see Sally. I really had the blahs, and I was ready to try anything.

Sally's office is on the second floor of the Doud Arcade on Ocean Avenue in Carmel, along with a couple of dentists and the publisher of one of those tourist pamphlets you find all over town. Downstairs is an assortment of shops that change character every few years, and an Italian restaurant that lends a garlicky atmosphere to the whole place.

"Morse Travel" was lettered in gold on the door, which I opened without knocking.

Seated at the only desk in the place was a woman I took to be Sally. As a matter of fact, it wasn't really a desk but a table. On a smaller table to the woman's left was a computer terminal. Before her were papers in neat piles. A third table against a side wall was covered with travel brochures. Huge posters covered the wall, extolling the virtues of Gstaad, Singapore, Bermuda, and other exotic, far-flung Shangri La's.

She rose from her chair and came around in front of her table-desk.

"How can I help you?" she asked with a practiced, businesslike smile.

Sally's hair is dark auburn honestly streaked with gray. Her jaw is strong and a bit too wide. She has green eyes that can light up when she's happy or laser you into cinders when she's angry. Her figure is full in the right places, but narrow at the waist. She's five-ten in heels and we just about see eye to eye. A formidable lady. As the French say, *for-mi-dah-bluh.*

I stood in her office trying to think what to say.

She spoke again: "Are you sure you're in the right place?"

"George Spelvin said you'd take care of me. I'm tired and bored."

"George did? Did he say I ran a massage parlor?"

"No, no, no. Please. George said you were the greatest travel agent in the world. A therapist."

Sally burst out laughing. She leaned back against her table and laughed loud and long. When she recovered, she said:

"You have made my day, mister. Forgive the Clintville cliche. Do you really want to go somewhere? Here, sit down. We'll talk."

We talked for an hour. About who I was and how I got to Carmel. And who she was and how she'd become the travel agent to the best people. When the phone rang and cut off our conversation, we had learned a lot about each other. We met for dinner that night at La Playa and filled in more of the details. We saw each other every day for a week, and on Friday we went home to my place at Sixth and Santa Rita for the weekend.

A whirlwind, passionate affair between two middle-aged people? Not really, my friends. There is some passion, in a relaxed, controlled sort of way. But Sally and I like each other. We are good friends. The fact that we're lovers is a fortuitous bonus.

Anyway, two weeks after we met, we went off to Maui together. And we've been involved in what the younger generation insists on calling a "relationship" ever since.

Sally lives in Carmel Valley, in a condo behind the Mid-Valley Shopping Center. It's a lot warmer and sunnier in the Valley during the summer months, but on the other hand, colder and kind of frosty in the winter.

"I can't stand the summer fog on the Peninsula," she has told me more than once. "I've got to see the sun and feel the warmth."

Of course, her office is in the fog belt, and she spends an occasional night or weekend with me. But in the summer, most evenings after work, she scurries home to the valley to "thaw out."

Her spirits began to rise as we turned off Highway One into the Carmel Valley Road.

"How've ya been, Riordan. Anything exciting happen while I was gone? Have you been true to me in your fashion?"

I told her the whole story of Reiko's experience with the mystery weekend debacle. Then I told her about Stewart Leonard's disappearance. She looked at me curiously when I mentioned Olin Vanderhof's name.

"My God, I've known Olin all my life. He and my dad were good friends. You know, the kind of family friend you're supposed to call 'uncle', even though you know damn well he's not. So Olin's in trouble. Well, I might have expected that."

I perked up. "What makes you say that?"

"Vanderhof? Olin Vanderhof? Tall, beautiful silver hair, late sixties, maybe seventy. Carries the world's sole surviving silver cigarette case? The Vanderhof Trust?"

"You've got it."

"Pat, I've done business with Olin and Emily for as long as I've been handling travel. For years I have arranged tours for them. Europe, God knows how many times. The Orient, South America—*everywhere*, Tibet, Sri Lanka. I always had carte blanche. They'd tell me what they wanted to do, I'd arrange it, always first class. Then little things began to happen. Slow pay. Bounced checks. Always made good, you understand. But the early signs of financial distress."

We arrived at Sally's condo. It's a pretty place, a cluster of buildings in a garden setting, quiet, no dogs, no kids, no swimming pool. Each unit has a small private patio, screened by tall shrubs. Sally likes to sun bathe in the buff upon occasion, ignoring my warnings about keratosis and skin cancer. "OK, so you won't join me. But you sure do like to look, sport."

I carried her bags into the living room, dropped them in the middle of the floor and sat down on the couch in simulated exhaustion. Sally threw her hat and jacket across the room, vaguely in the direction of a plush recliner, and sat on my lap.

She put her arms around my neck and gave me a long, lingering kiss.

"Sorry I was so crabby, Pat. I'm tired. It was a long, nasty trip. The food was terrible and it rained every day in Paris. I am weary and dirty and probably smell like I just set the track record at Churchill Downs. Why don't you get the hell back to Carmel while I soak four or five hours in a hot tub and get a good night's sleep?"

"Sally, you look great to me, and you smell like a very expensive French perfume that's gone a little rancid. I forgive you for your bitchiness. But I want to talk to you at some length about Olin Vanderhof."

"Not today, Patrick. Much too tired." She got off my lap and headed for the bedroom, unbuttoning her blouse. "Go home." She turned and struck a seductive pose. "Eat your heart out. And have a chat as soon as you can with Anson Ward."

"Who's Anson Ward?"

"He's the sweet little fellow who answers Olin's telephone. Private secretary to the Vanderhof Trust. Knows where all the bodies are buried. Try Anson."

13

"It was a terrible experience. . ."

REPORT FROM THE TECHNICAL ADVISOR (a clever reconstruction):

Reiko had called every hostelry on the Monterey Peninsula, from Carmel to Marina, without results. She called Ventana and the River Inn in Big Sur. Finally, when Motel 6 in Salinas informed her that none of the people she was looking for were registered there, she gave up in disgust after nearly four hours.

Making a mental note to charge all these message units to me, she started calling the homes of the Kesslers and the Caravellis in San Francisco, the Fowlers in Mill Valley, and the Shepherds in Sunnyvale.

Nobody home in Sunnyvale. In Mill Valley, a small, very polite voice answered, "Fowler residence, Alan speaking," and told Reiko that "mummy and daddy are away for the weekend" and offered to take a message. Reiko, a little stunned, left her number and added, "Say hello to George Lucas for me, will you?"

Her next call was answered by machine, a big voice, filled with self-amusement. "Hello, this is Stan Kessler. I'm sorry I can't answer the phone, but I'm in bed with a couple of UCLA cheerleaders who wanna know the facts of life. (Muffled laughter in the background.) When you hear the beep, leave your name and number. I'll call you back if I got the strength."

Reiko slammed down the receiver angrily and whispered,

"Shithead!"

She punched the last set of numbers viciously. The phone at the other end rang twice and then: "Joe Caravelli." It was a mild, quiet voice, patient and a little tired.

Reiko was flustered. She didn't know quite what to say.

"Mr. Caravelli, this is Reiko Masuda. You don't know me, but I am working for the people who put on the mystery weekend in Monterey. I'm sorry to disturb you on a Sunday, but I need to get some information."

There was a silence on the line for several seconds. Mr. Caravelli was probably trying to formulate a response.

"Miss Masuda, my wife and I left Monterey just after talking to the police. It was a terrible experience, and we just thought we'd be more comfortable at home. Don't bother about the refund. We really don't need the money. There's nothing I can tell you."

Reiko persisted: "Mr. Caravelli, did you know the man who was killed...Mr. Levine?"

A longer silence at the other end.

"I told the police we were old acquaintances. That's true. But there's more. I guess it's going to come out sooner or later. Harry and Gene Fowler and I, well, we had some business connections. We needed to meet in the Monterey area to look into what might be a serious emergency, and this murder wing-ding seemed like a pretty good cover. Very sensitive business, banking. Can't alarm the depositors. We were going to get together Saturday—God, was that yesterday?—and talk about the problem with some other people. But I don't know who got to Harry...or why."

Reiko's heartbeat had quickened when Caravelli answered the phone and it was racing now. She tried to be calm.

"Mr. Caravelli, can you tell me the names of your business associates in the Monterey area? They might be able to help us...and the police."

"I don't know if I should. Maybe I've told you too much already. You aren't even official, are you?"

Reiko caught her breath, but lied bravely onward: "I am a private investigator working for the promoters of the mystery weekend, Mr. Caravelli. Anything you tell me is in confidence."

Pause. A tapping sound, as of the drumming of a pencil against a desk top.

Caravelli spoke slowly: "All of us—Levine and Fowler and I—are shareholders in a small banking enterprise in Hollister—"

"The Farmers' and Ranchers'?"

The man in San Francisco stammered in surprise: "Y-yes, that's the one. How'd you—? Well, it doesn't matter. The man we do business with mainly is a fellow named..."

"Olin Vanderhof?"

Caravelli gasped. "Oh, Jesus, how many other people know about this bank business? Is it all over the Peninsula? We don't even know what it's all about yet. Except that the bank manager has run out, and Vanderhof's accountants are examining the books."

"It's all in confidence, Mr. Caravelli, all in confidence." Reiko was experiencing a tightness in the throat, indicating that she was growing elated with the information she had just acquired. But, more importantly, she was particularly gleeful that she was one up on me at this point.

14

"The Vanderhof millions and the Warren millions would be...down the drain, don't you know."

THE OFFICES OF THE VANDERHOF TRUST are in a rambling one-story adobe on Calle Principal in Monterey. There's a mustiness about the place that hits you when you enter. It's furnished—appropriately—in 18th Century Spanish-type furniture made in a small factory in 20th Century Seaside, California. It is decorated with candelabra and crossed sabers, and oil paintings of unidentified glowering Spanish aristocrats. The place has a funereal gloom about it. I got a little chill as I crossed the threshold.

Sitting at a massive oak table in the anteroom was a young man I took to be Anson Ward. He seemed engrossed in what appeared to be a legal document. I estimated his age at anywhere between thirty and forty. He had a strange transparent look, thinning pale yellow hair, and skin through which I could trace a network of fine blue blood vessels.

When he became aware of my presence and looked up, I could see that his eyes were heavy-lidded, with only the bottom semi-circle of iris showing. The whole picture was one of effeteness, a world-weary attitude.

Ward smiled faintly. "Yes?"

"I'm Pat Riordan. To see Mr. Vanderhof."

"Ah, yes, Mr. Riordan. I'm terribly sorry. Mr. Vanderhof is golfing this morning. At Pebble. Is there anything I can help you with? I'm Anson Ward, Mr. Vanderhof's private secretary."

"Maybe you *can* help me, Anson. You must know why Mr. Vanderhof hired me, so I won't get into that at all. I'm looking for Stewart Leonard. But a friend of mine has suggested that Mr. Vanderhof may be having some financial problems, so I—"

"A friend?"

"Sally Morse."

"Ah, yes, Sally. Dear girl. Lots of fun. Talks out of turn now and then. Too often."

He placed the document he had been reading neatly on the desk, carefully squaring the edges and aligning them with the rectangle of the desk top.

"I...am...not...at liberty to give you any details of Mr. Vanderhof's financial situation. But I suspect that if you are as thoroughgoing as Mr. Spelvin has told us, you'll eventually turn up some rather disagreeable facts.

"The Vanderhof Trust was formed to conserve the assets owned by Mr. Vanderhof himself, of course, and those of his wife. She was Emily Warren, whose family owned a rather large part of Carmel Valley.

"In recent years, certain financial reverses have made it necessary to sell off a substantial amount of property and reinvest the proceeds. Mainly it was the bank, that ugly little building over in Hollister that was performing like a gold mine until now.

"I don't know the exact numbers, Mr. Riordan. I do know that the Vanderhof Trust, when formed, was worth perhaps a hundred million. It is now, ah, somewhat diminished."

"Diminished?"

"Without the bank shares, it would be—to coin a phrase—in a negative state, Mr. Riordan. The Vanderhof millions and the Warren millions would be...down the drain, don't you know."

All this from a guy who was "not at liberty" to give me any details. I am sure not going to tell Anson any secrets.

Ward pushed himself back from the desk and stood up. He is a small man, small-boned, with delicate hands which he uses too gracefully. And when I saw him in profile, I noticed that his chin was set back about a half-inch from his bite.

"But I have told you too much already, Mr. Riordan." That might have been an understatement. "However, I have been expecting any day for the shit—what *is* the expression?—to hit the fan, as it were. It isn't as if I haven't had any other job offers. But I've grown rather fond of this office. Decorated it myself. Don't you like it, Mr. Riordan? Doesn't it just bring out the conquistador in you?"

"Maybe a little more like the Cisco Kid, Anson. Don't worry. I will not divulge anything you've told me to the wrong people. Thanks very much. And have a good day."

I was glad to be out in the fresh air and sunshine of Monterey. The damp mustiness of Vanderhof's office, tinged with the scent of Ward's cologne, and the presence of the threatening, anonymous Spaniards on the walls all tended to depress me. There's a little walkway between Calle Principal and Alvarado Street that ends between two restaurants just across the street from my office. I jaywalked across and climbed the stairs.

Reiko was sitting on her heels on the tatami mat in her cramped little half-room, looking smug.

"As my old Virginia grandma used to say, little one, you look like the cat that ate the canary," I said, rather patronizingly.

"Riordan, it is coming together. *Your* and *my* case are our case."

"You mean where everybody knows everybody else and nobody can figure it out but Angela Lansbury?"

She glared at me. You have never been glared at until Reiko has glared at you.

"Why do you insist on being such a smartass bastard all the time? Why do you get such a kick out of putting me down?"

I flinched. "Reiko-san, I apologize. I don't get a kick out of putting you down...and I *do* need a kick in the ass."

She sniffed and looked at me sideways through her narrowed eyes. When she concluded that I was sufficiently contrite, she told me about the phone calls and the gospel according to Caravelli.

I then brought her up to date on the Vanderhof situation.

"So-o-o-o," she said. "These three guys—Caravelli, Levine, and Fowler—were using the mystery weekend as a convenient cover for a meeting about the Farmers' and Ranchers' Bank. And before they could meet, somebody killed Levine. But where the hell is Stewart

Leonard?"

"Well, honey, it's pretty obvious that Leonard's disappearance is tied in tight with the whole mess. When we turn up some word on him, we'll be in the home stretch."

Reiko bounded up from the mat and began moving thoughtfully around her desk, patting her computer, straightening out her pencil jar, adjusting pictures on the wall. I was lounging in the door that leads to my office. She stopped squarely in front of me, and faced me as nearly as she could from five-feet-nothing.

"You say you need me, Pat. You say I mean so much to you, and that you depend on me. Yet you sometimes treat me like a fifteen-year old virgin. Why is that?"

That took me by surprise. Reiko, as I've said before, has been with me for ten years, which would make her about thirty-five. She simply does not age. Also, as I have said, I owe her my life. She arrived at just the right moment to pull me out of a steep dive. I've always been a little bit (or maybe more) in love with her. But it hadn't occurred to me. . . .

"I am a grown woman, Pat. With all the emotions and all the equipment. I have men friends other than you, and some of them have spent the night at my flat. You've been aware of my dates—but when one comes to the office, you size him up like a prospective son-in-law. I haven't found anybody I would consider marrying. I. . .I. . .I've always been very fond of you. But you treat me like a little girl."

I hugged her close. Ten years. All kinds of situations. A certain kind of love. I smoothed her hair, and her tears made a big wet spot on my shirt.

"Forgive me, Reiko-san. I'm getting old and stupid. Or maybe stupidly getting old."

She snuffled into my chest and drew back. That irresistible smile was returning.

"Love ya, Riordan. But I have to go to the john. I've got a lunch date in a half hour and my face is ruined."

She pulled away and dashed out of the room, pulling tissues from a box on her desk and loudly blowing her nose.

For a long moment, I felt insanely jealous. Then sheepish, like

Jimmy Carter must have felt when he made that crack to *Playboy* about lusting in his heart.

For the first time in my life I felt twenty years too old.

15

Mysterious, anonymous callers usually leave me cold.

I DUG THE LEONARD FILE OUT of my desk drawer and flipped it open. This man is the key to the whole bloody situation, I thought. He's the one human being who can tie everything together. But where the hell is he?

Vanderhof had not reported the man missing in San Benito County. He was worried about the story getting around and having some effect on the bank. But the man was a resident of Monterey County. Maybe I could get a little sneaky on this one.

I called the Sheriff's substation on Aguajito Road and asked for Tony Balestreri.

After a couple of switches, he came on: "Balestreri. Speak!"

"Pat Riordan, Tony. How are you?"

"Riordan, this has been a fine, quiet, sunshiny Monterey day so far. No murders so far. No murders in the county, no grand larceny, not even a fender-bender at the airport turn-off. Now, what are you going to lay on me?"

"Sergeant, I don't always bring you bad news. I have occasionally bought you lunch. In my modest fashion, I have even helped you in your work."

"Bag up the fertilizer, Pat. What do you want?"

"I happen to know that a citizen in your jurisdiction has mysteriously disappeared. I am not at liberty to identify the guy for reasons that will become apparent at a later date. I am used to

tracking down errant husbands, wives and offspring. But this subject is not in one of those categories. He's a single business man, a
banker, without a negative mark on his record who seems to have
locked the door to his condo and walked into the Twilight Zone."

"Pat, you know that I have to tell you officially that if the man
has been missing for a considerable length of time and the possibility
of foul play exists, the case should be turned over to the authorities,
meaning *us*. Since I know you're not going to do that, all I can tell
you is that you are in big trouble. If a man without close family ties
decides to leave for reasons other than criminal, he is unrestrained,
he can split. Depending on how long he has been gone, he could be
in Montreal, Karachi, or the Carmel Highlands. He probably has a
car and he probably left in it. The car has a license plate, and if *we*
had the number, we'd put it and a description on the missing
persons network and hope for the best. Say, *has* this guy committed
some kind of crime? Is that why you're being so damned secretive?"

"If I knew for sure he had done something wrong, I'd give you the
whole scoop right now. There's a possibility. But my client doesn't
know yet."

"Sounds like a possible absconder. Key man missing. Funds
maybe missing. Hanky-panky at the banky."

Balestreri's idea of humor often grates on my finer sensibilities,
but he is a gifted cop.

"I'll be in touch, Tony," I said, and hung up.

There are times when I wish I could just lie back in my big
upholstered swivel chair and put my feet up on the desk and shut
out the noises of the world. In this position and under these
conditions, I could perhaps drift off into a dream that would present
to me all of the known facts of a problem in perfectly logical order.
At the conclusion of this reverie there would come the blinding
flash of intuition that reveals the perfect solution.

It has never really worked that way. I lie back in the chair and I go
to sleep sometimes, but when I wake up I'm no smarter than I was.

Let's see, now. Do it chronologically. Has to go like this: Vanderhof Trust is in trouble for reasons unknown. Bad management, most
likely. Too often inherited fortunes are pissed away by heirs who
aren't especially astute. So Olin Vanderhof, down to his last million

or so, liquidates everything and puts it into bank stock. He has to take in partners, so he goes to my buddy George Spelvin and the three mystery fans, Fowler, Levine and Caravelli. And the other guy, Barry Heathcote, whoever he is. Maybe more.

Anyway, they hire Stew Leonard to manage. All goes well for five or six years. Everything is serene and the bottom line is growing more and more positive.

Then, Stew Leonard is gone without saying good-bye to anybody and Olin Vanderhof is in a panic. He alerts his directors and three of them show up on this crazy mystery weekend in Monterey, during which, according to Caravelli, they were going to do some serious talking. But before the conference can happen, somebody kills Levine.

Levine's date for the weekend is Stew Leonard's sister who is, no matter what she says, an expensive hooker.

Coincidence? Maybe the answer to that is part of the key. At this point, I dozed off.

I was jerked out of an idyllic dream in which I was boating down the Rhine in perfect weather, gazing at incredible castles on green peaks. This must have come from hanging around Sally Morse's office looking at travel posters. Might have been Freudian. Might have been Sally's hills and valleys. Oh, well, no matter.

The raucous sound that brought me abruptly home was the telephone on my desk. It's one of those new ones for which some sadistic engineer has devised a signal that suggests a Siamese cat fight.

Reiko was gone—to lunch, I guess—so I picked up the phone. "H'lo. Riordan here."

The voice on the other end was barely more than a whisper.

"If you are interested in finding out more about Stewart Leonard, come to cottage number eight at the Carmel River Inn at three o'clock this afternoon. You might say . . . it's a matter of life and death . . . to more than one. Three o'clock." A click, and the dial tone.

I looked at my watch. It was one-thirty.

Mysterious, anonymous callers usually leave me cold. But they don't ring me up every day. There was, however, a sense of urgency in that voice that I simply could not ignore. Besides, how many people knew I was looking for Stewart Leonard?

16

...a neat small-caliber bullet in her forehead....

I SCRIBBLED A NOTE TO REIKO:

"A startling development has presented itself. If I do not return, make positive to lock the door when you leave. V.T. Yrs., H. Poirot."

Then I walked across the street to the Poppy for a sandwich and a cup of coffee. Hell, I wasn't just being cool. I was hungry.

If you ever happen into this little restaurant, find a table in the back where you can appreciate some of the finer small paintings of the late S.C. Yuan, an artist of transcendant skill and vitality. I've got one of his paintings, purchased at just the right time. Some years ago, Yuan, feeling that his creative life was at an end, was a suicide. His paintings now bring high prices. Mine is worth big bucks now, but I wouldn't part with it.

The artist's daughter owns this little restaurant, but it's a cinch that ninety percent of her customers have no idea of the quality of these paintings. You might say, if you were so disposed, "*sic transit gloria mundi.*" Or, "I don't know anything about art, but I know what I like."

Why three o'clock? Why did the whispering voice say three o'clock? When I finished my club sandwich (the bacon was a trifle underdone) it was nearly half past two, and at this time of day it couldn't take more than fifteen minutes to go over the hill to Carmel and down to the Inn by the Carmel River where I used to stay many times before I moved to the Peninsula. It's a place you have to know about. From the road, all you see is a conventional two-story motel. But back beyond the motel with it's tiny swimming pool is a cluster of cottages nestled in the trees, some fairly new, some very old. Helen and I spent many a quiet night in one or another of those cottages. I had never thought of it before, but it's a great place to hide out.

On such an occasion as this, when you're meeting somebody you don't know at the invitation of an obviously disguised voice, you don't jump the gun. That's just an expression. I don't like guns. Very strange, you say, for a man in my profession. So you got me. They're never going to do my life on TV. I guess I saw too many bodies destroyed by gunshot in Korea. I could never hit anybody with a hand gun anyhow. In the Army I tried to qualify with a GI forty-five. I would have been just as effective heaving the thing at the target.

I took the long way around, the scenic route through Pacific Grove: Ocean View to Sunset Drive to Forest, and up over the Holman Highway to Highway One. The traffic was flowing nicely on the stretch from the top of the Carmel Hill south. In the summer time it stacks up at the top of Ocean Avenue in Carmel because the tourists know only one way to get at the irresistible goodies in the village: the Clint T-shirts, the clever bumper stickers, the chocolate chip cookies.

The light was green at Rio Road and I turned into Oliver and the entrance to the Carmel River Inn just at three. Minding the speed bumps carefully, I pulled up in front of cottage number eight.

There was no car in the narrow carport, nor any parked nearby. The shutters were closed, and there was an ominous quiet about the place. I sat for a moment and thought. It was highly unlikely that there was a bad guy in there waiting to open up on me with a .357 magnum. I remembered the Prince in *War and Peace*. What did he say? "Why are they shooting at *me*? Everybody *loves* me?" I didn't know anything, and there wasn't any reason to think I did. So I got out of the car, walked up to the door, and knocked.

Silence. I knocked again. No response. I called out: "Hello in there." Nothing.

The knob turned easily in my hand, and I pushed the door open. In the small room there were twin beds. On the nearer one, with her hands gracefully arranged in a cross at her breastbone, her dress neatly draped as if she were posed for an exotic perfume ad, with a neat small-caliber bullet hole in her forehead, was the beautiful escort, Shirley Leonard.

17

"Don't be so goddam delicate, Riordan.
She was a whore, right?"

"**H**ER CAR IS PARKED up on Oliver. Looks like she either didn't know the street was closed at the motel entrance, or maybe she'd been told to park outside and walk in." Tony Balestreri was sitting on the bed recently vacated by Shirley Leonard's corpse. I sat on the other bed, feeling and probably looking a little bewildered.

Balestreri grinned. "Well, now, Patrick, you've got to tell me just what you know about this homicide. You found it. Why the hell were you here?"

I mumbled something about privileged information and confidentiality, but Balestreri was right. I had to tell him some of the story, if not all.

"You do remember, Sergeant, that I asked you about a missing person thing I was working on. Well, this lady was the missing person's long lost sister. What I mean is, they hadn't seen each other for years because the brother didn't approve of the sister's profession, if you know what I mean."

"Don't be so goddam delicate, Riordan. She was a whore, right? But why was she here if he didn't give a damn about her? She was in a two hundred dollar a night suite at the Plaza. She had about fifteen hundred bucks worth of clothes on. She had eight hundred and some change in her purse, and every credit card known to man. She must have been the 'prostitute with a heart of gold' that I've always heard about but never found, to want to see her brother that badly, when he probably thought she was a piece of shit."

I just sat there and looked dumb. Balestreri and I had been all over the little cottage looking for anything that might give us something to go on. The place was clean. The paper strip was still over the toilet. The room clerk had told us that the woman had taken the room herself at about eleven-thirty that morning. He remembered that she had asked if a message had been left for her. It hadn't. But somebody must have known she'd be here. Who?

Well, now I had a murder case to match Reiko's. And the relationship of one to the other was almost too obvious to be true. Shirley had come to Monterey with Harry Levine. Harry was a weekend trick—she would have said "client"— and Harry was found dead in a hotel room with a neat little hole between his eyes.

Not long after that deplorable incident, Shirley Leonard was found in another hotel room (still hauntingly beautiful), with that ever-so-precise hole to match Harry's.

Balestreri ran some yellow tape around the cottage, and told the office that number eight was off limits for a while.

I was sitting in the Mercedes, thinking it badly needed a paint job, and about to turn the key, when he appeared at the window.

He spoke softly, but with determination: "I'm not going to push you at this moment, Pat. But sooner or later, I'm going to have to hear all you know about this thing."

He banged his hand on the top of my car, and walked away.

Coming out of the Carmel River Inn onto Highway One takes real courage. The narrow bridge across the river is on your right, and with the speedy flow of traffic from the north, you can't get far enough out to see what's coming from the south. What you've got, you see, is a kind of automotive Russian roulette. Out of what I prefer to call discretion rather than cowardice, I often turn right, and run as far as the park entrance at Point Lobos to turn around and come back. The traffic on a summer weekend is often backed up that far back from the Rio Road traffic light, bumper to bumper, moving a few inches at a time.

But on the day of Shirley Leonard's murder, in the relative quiet of November, I pulled boldly out and swung left, accelerating in haste as the driver of a utility truck coming over the bridge hit his brakes and sent a stream of obscenities after me.

Over the hill to Monterey. The day was clear, and I could see the blue bay from the highway, a sight that almost always gives me pleasure. But I felt a strange sort of depression. The feeling wasn't new to me. However, it usually meant that I was guiltily aware that I had missed something critical.

When I got to the office it was after five, and Reiko was gone. On the door, secured with a piece of scotch tape, was a note written in Japanese. She likes to do that, knowing that as far as I am concerned, it might as well be in Sanskrit or Tocharian. There *was* a P.S. in English: "Some new stuff maybe on O.V. Don't call me, I'll call you. Or I'll see you in the morning. R. Masuda, technical advisor."

18

"I'm a pretty good old girl, really."

NEXT MORNING I was in the office before the technical advisor showed up. I had arisen early, taken a needle shower, or what passed for one in the remodeled bathroom of my charming Carmel house that dates from the twenties. A slight miscalculation in the placement of the tub causes part of the shower water to go out the window. It had been with a surge of optimism and a strong will that I drove over to Monterey to challenge the day.

I sat at my desk, drinking coffee from the bakery downstairs, munching on a chocolate stuffed croissant, a delicacy I have come to love, but which, I suspect, would make a self-respecting Parisian ill.

The lady who walked rather shyly into my office took me quite by surprise, causing me to hastily wipe my greasy fingers on the sports section of the *Herald*, and rise clumsily to my feet.

"Mr. Riordan, I am Emily Vanderhof. You know my husband."

I thought, "God, she must have been beautiful when she was young." But then I realized, with some shame, that she was still beautiful: sixties beautiful, not twenties beautiful.

She had short, perfectly groomed white hair, and smooth, unlined skin, without any suggestion of surgical adjustment. Her eyes were clear and bright, and her modest smile won me completely. This is the woman George Spelvin described as "homely"? George, the connoisseur of feminine beauty, the collector of a showcase full of cover girls? Goddam! Too many rich people got no taste.

"Please sit down, Mrs. Vanderhof."

She sat in the chair her husband had occupied just a few days before. The clothes she wore were such an essential part of the whole picture that you didn't notice them. I cannot remember what she wore that day. Emily Vanderhof presented such an impression of exquisite good taste that I immediately felt my chin to see if I had shaved closely enough, straightened my tie, and checked to see if my fly was zipped.

Emily looked at me curiously for the better part of a minute.

"You don't look like a private detective, Mr. Riordan. You appear to be a rather nice man. A bit older than I had expected, though. I can't quite see you in a barroom brawl with a bad guy. But I can see why Sally is attracted to you. Are you good in bed, Mr. Riordan?"

I could feel this deep flush creeping up the back of my neck and spreading around into my face. She knew that Sally and I are ...well, intimate friends. The query about my skills as a lover was disconcerting coming from that lovely, serene face.

The bright blue eyes twinkled, and Emily smiled broadly.

"Oh, don't be embarrassed, Mr. Riordan. That's just my way. I love to say startling things to people and watch them react. Let's say it comes from many years of associating with my own and my husband's stuffy society friends. I love nothing better than to upset people at dinner parties. There's no meanness to it. I just startle them a bit and watch them squirm."

She reached across the desk and put her hand on mine.

"Don't be put off, Mr. Riordan. I'm a pretty good old girl, really. When Olin told me that George Spelvin had suggested a private investigator to him, I was a bit suspicious. I got a vision of a shifty-eyed individual in a seedy trenchcoat. We've known George for ages, but he is a little bit...eccentric. You look to me like a kind and reasonable man. And Sally's no fool."

She sat back in the chair.

"Olin is terribly worried about this business at the bank. Stewart Leonard's disappearance was a terrible shock. My husband has always been such a, well, tower of strength, an unavoidable cliche. He has kept a youthful outlook. He runs, swims, plays tennis, golf. I've always believed him to be practically *indestructible*—like the live oak trees. We have so many of them around here, Mr. Riordan, just as we have many older residents on the Peninsula. The live oaks grow old and twisted and ugly, but they're strong. They endure the oak worms and the oak moths, but they survive. Not that I think of Olin as old and twisted and ugly. I think he's quite a handsome man, don't you?"

I had been staring at this lovely woman with my mouth open, like an adenoidal adolescent.

"Yes, ma'am," I said, in a tone I might have used to my sixth grade teacher, Miss Beckwith, who wore pince nez spectacles and scared the hell out of me, "Mr. Vanderhof is a, uh, striking figure." Whatever that meant.

A small veil of sadness came over Mrs. Vanderhof's eyes.

"If you are really a good detective, Mr. Riordan, as good as George and Olin think you are, then you are likely to turn up some pretty disagreeable facts about our family. And you may discover that Olin is in rather serious...financial distress."

She fingered a brooch on the lapel of her jacket. For a moment, her gaze shifted to the window behind my left shoulder.

"Olin does not know that *I* know of his money troubles. He has always protected me that way. But we've lived together a long time, and I can read him well, Mr. Riordan. He is a sweet, dear, gentle man—but not very good at business, I'm afraid. When it became obvious to me that Olin was in trouble, I talked to Anson. I dislike the sneaky little bastard, but he is quite bright and he knows... too much."

Somehow her use of the word "bastard" in Anson's case didn't detract a bit from this dear lady's dignity. For Anson it was a very good word. At that moment, I might have thought of a better one, some sort of unflattering anatomical reference. But, as I learned later on, "bastard" was a *very* good word for Anson Ward.

"This brings me to the reason for my visit. No matter what you discover, you must never allow my husband to know that *I* know about the loss of the better part of our holdings. Olin loves me dearly, and I am devoted to him." She averted her eyes. "He...has never done anything *intentionally* to hurt anybody. He couldn't. Will you help me, Mr. Riordan?"

I could not refuse this lady anything. But I had some reservations. "I will do what I can, ma'am. But I'm a little confused. Why do you come to me? Anson's more likely to spill the beans. He seems like the type who'd get a charge out of crossing somebody. Maybe especially you."

She smiled a saintly smile.

"Mr. Riordan, Anson and I have a clear...understanding. He won't betray me. Please, just promise me that you won't tell Olin that I'm aware of his...our...financial misfortunes."

"OK, Mrs. Vanderhof—but you must make me a promise." "Oh...what?"

"If you learn anything at all about the sudden disappearance of Stewart Leonard, you'll let me know."

"Done!" she said. Emily Vanderhof arose from her chair and extended her hand. Her handshake was firm and brisk. She smiled again, and the twinkle returned to her eyes.

"Give my love to Sally," she said, as she walked out my office door.

19

"That was before he started looking like an iguana."

REIKO WALKED IN seconds later, wide-eyed.

"Who was that gorgeous woman, Riordan? I saw her come out the door as I came to the top of the stairs."

"That, Reiko-san, was the beloved wife of our Mr. Vanderhof. She paid me a visit to ask politely that I not let her husband know that *she* knows he's almost broke. He's proud and protective, you see. Hasn't told her a thing about his troubles. But you can't fool a wife you've lived with a few years. She always knows what you're thinking—sometimes before you do."

That old emptiness came back for just a moment. Helen had been gone more than ten years. But we had about that many years together, and the hurt is still there, down deep.

I pushed the past out of my mind.

"How was the lunch date, honey?"

"Bad, Riordan. I mean the food was good. We went to that place that overlooks Fisherman's Wharf. It's the date that was bad. Friend of Amy's. Nerdy. I had three glasses of wine to ease the boredom. When I got back here I was sozzled. But . . . ask me what happened to sober me up."

"Later, honey. I've got to make a phone call."

From the look on her face, I suspected that she was about to tell me to perform a physically impossible act. But she just glared murderously, tilted her nose in the air, and went directly to her computer.

Later, baby. I was going to have to find out more about Anson Ward. I had seen him there in Vanderhof's office, a smirking little man with heavy-lidded eyes. But Emily Vanderhof's visit had sharpened my interest in Anson.

I called George Spelvin. I invariably call George for the dirt on people. George is sort of the *National Enquirer* of Pebble Beach.

"Anson? Why do you need to know about that little twit? He's an oily type, Patrick. Gives me the creeps. I don't go to Olin's office very often just because of Anson. Being in the same room with him spooks me."

"Hell, George, he *seems* harmless."

"Probably is. But you know how some people feel about spiders or snakes. That's how I feel about Anson."

"How'd he get the job with Vanderhof?"

"He's Emily's nephew. Didn't you know that? Maybe 'nephew' is the wrong word. Y'see, Emily had a younger brother who was what we used to call a 'black sheep', remember? He was your typical aimless rich kid, spoiled rotten. He dedicated his life to fast cars, booze, and women."

"George, that's a stereotype if I ever heard one. Did you know the guy?"

"Oh, sure. He was a complete charmer, lots of fun at a party. Away from parties, totally irresponsible."

"Did he have a job? Did he ever work?"

"Come on now, Riordan. Sure, he worked about as much as I do. Running errands for his father when the old man was alive. When Harley Warren, Sr., checked out, the boy just settled back on his share of the estate. Meanwhile, Emily had married Olin and left the Warren home in the Valley. So Harley, Jr., had it all to himself."

"Let's get back to Anson, George."

"I was coming to that. Harley had dedicated his life, as I said, to booze and sexual intercourse. And fast cars. And, believe it or not, they all ganged up and killed him. He wasn't particular about the women he went to bed with. There were a lot of girls anxious to oblige him. He was reasonably good-looking, and God knows he had plenty of money. They came and went, those women, if you'll forgive my little dirty joke." I could almost see the leer on George's face. He has affected a clipped mustache and a van dyke beard during the past year or so, managing to look even more devilish than when I first met him.

He went on: "But one weekend, Harley met this kind of homely little redhead over in Salinas. I've got no idea what he was doing in Salinas. Anyhow, he went home with her, and she must have been pretty special, because he stayed with her a week. As I remember the story, he woke up in the middle of the night, figured out where he was, left without waking the woman, and started back to Monterey. He must have been doing eighty when he had a head-on with a truck near Laguna Seca. There wasn't much left of him or the guy in the pickup."

"Don't tell me, George. The redhead was pregnant. The baby turned out to be Anson."

"You've got it. The woman raised the kid by herself to school age. Then she came to see Emily, who had inherited Harley's share of their father's estate. She wanted out. The kid was beginning to be a burden and a bore. His mother was looking for a little freedom and excitement. Emily insisted on some tests to prove the kid was Harley's. But she was pretty well convinced that the kid was a Warren. He looked like her brother. That was before he started looking like an iguana."

"Then Emily took him in?"

"In a way. Emily sent him to boarding school. She and Olin had their own kids to look after and she didn't want Anson around to remind her of her brother. As far as the Vanderhof kids were concerned, Anson was the offspring of a 'friend' of their mother's who had been killed in an automobile accident. He had been given his mother's name. And I don't think even Anson was aware of just who he was until his mother visited him at USC. After that, he began to put the pressure on Emily."

"That's when he got to be Olin's secretary?"

"No, not right away. Emily got him a job when he finished college in a friend's business. He blew it in a hurry. Antagonized everybody, stole money. Just a consummate jerk. She got him two or three other jobs. Same pattern. Finally, she talked Olin into taking him in.

He was just as sneaky as ever, but, hell, it was all in the family."

"Thanks, George. You've been a lot of help. I think."

I sat back in my chair. "Talk to Anson," Sally had said. She must know the whole messy story. I didn't press the guy hard enough on our first meeting. I'd pay him another call. I wasn't sure about how to open the conversation, but....

He was spraying water from an atomizer on some potted plants with dark green leaves when I arrived.

"Mr. Riordan, how nice to see you again. Mr. Vanderhof is out, I'm afraid." He gave me that smirk again, a sort of smile, a sort of cross between Mona Lisa and Alfred E. Neuman.

"Came to talk to *you*, Anson. Got a minute?"

"I was just about to go to lunch, Mr. Riordan. Would you care to accompany me? I hate to eat alone."

"Good enough. Where?"

"There's a place I like just down the street. In the old firehouse. I recommend it, Mr. Riordan."

Anson carefully checked the office, making sure, I guess, that everything was in the right place. For the first time, I became aware of the fact that the office had no windows. It was well ventilated, air-conditioned no doubt, but completely sealed from outside light. When the lights were turned off it would be totally dark, like a bank vault.

Anson locked the door and we walked north on Calle Principal to the restaurant. It *was* in a refurbished firehouse, complete with sliding pole, full of young professional men and women, all talking. The sound level in a place like this compounds itself. Everybody has to talk a little louder to be heard over the general din. Consequently, at the lunch hour, the decibels begin on a reasonable level at about eleven-thirty, and increase to merely ear-splitting at one o'clock. After that there is a tapering off.

Everybody seemed to know Anson. He must grab a lot of checks, I thought. The hostess led us to a table in a relatively quiet corner and whisked away a small "reserved" sign.

"They know me here," said Anson, obviously pleased. "They hold this table until 12:15. That's why I was in a bit of a rush."

We ordered: a club sandwich for me, a spinach quiche for

Anson, coffee for both.

"Well," he said, as our waitperson (What a ridiculous word!) slipped away, "what's on your mind, Mr. Riordan?"

"Anson, George Spelvin has told me something of your background. It appears that you are tighter with the Vanderhofs than I would have imagined."

"Oh, that old story. Everybody knows it, Mr. Riordan. Monterey's a small town, full of gossipy people." He paused and closed his eyes, recalling the data and delivering it in a flat, mechanical voice. "Monterey, 31,000 last census. Pacific Grove, 18,000. Carmel, under 5,000, and I don't think anybody knows how many people live in Pebble Beach. They're so *inbred* over there." Anson brushed something off the table and began to study the silverware.

"Anson, I need your help. What can you tell me about Olin Vanderhof's business associates?"

"Nothing."

"Nothing?"

He looked directly at me with that hooded reptilian gaze.

"I am a confidential secretary, Mr. Riordan. I cannot divulge facts about my employer's business. Ah, here we are."

The waitress had arrived with our lunch. Anson must swing a lot of weight here, I thought. I had never been served so fast. Either they had a lot of respect for him, or they wanted to get rid of him. I wasn't sure which.

We ate in silence. Anson gobbled his quiche. It seemed to evaporate under his fork. He managed to accompany his meal with great chunks of French bread slathered with butter. It was a spectacle. I watched in utter fascination, toying with my sandwich which had arrived full of sprouts. I hate sprouts.

The check arrived as hastily as had the meal. The waitress never bothered to check in with the perfunctory, "Well, how are things over here?", and the forced smile. Anson kept on eating as I laid the money down.

When he finished, he dabbed at his mouth with his napkin, took a final sip of his coffee, got up and moved toward the door. I followed, accidentally jostling our waitress who had zeroed in on the money. She rapidly calculated the tip and gave me a withering look.

Anson was out the door and walking briskly toward his office when I caught up with him.

"Oh, thank you, Mr. Riordan. I really didn't mean for you to pick up the tab. That was awfully nice." That miserable smile again. We walked swiftly until Anson stopped at his office door.

He put the key into the lock and grasped the door handle. But before he turned the key and opened the door, he faced me.

"I *can* tell you, Mr. Riordan, that things are not as they seem in the Vanderhof family. No, things are *not* as they seem. Bye-bye."

He opened the door quickly, and disappeared inside.

20

"Bring your samurai sword, kid."

Wﾍﾍ HEN I GOT BACK to the office, Reiko was stone-faced and full of righteous indignation. She wouldn't look at me.

"So what happened to sober you up, my friend?"

She shot me a venomous glance, and turned back to her computer.

"Really, honey, I'm interested. I'm sorry I had to run out on you. What the hell else can I say?"

She seemed to relax in her infernal knee-chair. She rose, smoothed out her skirt, and condescended to come to me. I could see that she was really bursting to tell me something. We walked into my office, and she began her little dance of excitement, her small feet moving in an Arthur Murray diagram, her hands describing Japanese characters in the air.

"I am sitting at my desk—after lunch, still a little sozzled—and in walks Eugene Fowler!"

"To that, Reiko-san, I say a rousing 'so what?' Who the hell is Eugene Fowler?"

"I worry about you, Pat. Eugene Fowler is the Marin County guy who is on the board of the Farmers' and Ranchers' Bank, along with Vanderhof, Caravelli—and the late Levine. Caravelli had called him. Fowler has this little getaway house in the Carmel Woods— something I hadn't even thought of when I was trying to find him—and he and his wife went there after the murder."

"My God, if Fowler had a place in Carmel, why didn't the board meet there in the first place?"

"Well, Levine had already signed up for the mystery weekend. And besides, the others knew all about Levine's weakness for professional ladies. I get the idea that Mrs. Fowler didn't approve of the guy anyhow, and didn't want him in her house. So the group went along with good old Harry."

I remembered something. "Does the name Barry Heathcote mean anything to you? Has anybody mentioned it?"

"Funny you should ask. Fowler did drop that name. Who...?"

"Never mind. Tell me about Fowler. What did he say?"

Reiko described vividly the arrival of Eugene Fowler:

He loomed in the doorway, a man of large proportions. His head barely cleared the door frame, and his shoulders brushed the wood on both sides. This is an old building, and these are generous doors. But Fowler took up a lot of space. The man must have weighed two-fifty or two-seventy-five. He had a thick head of black hair that looked too glossy to be legitimate, and a large puffy face that went with the body, and featured a nose that bulged slightly at the tip and a great wide mouth. He was smoking the biggest cigar Reiko had ever seen.

"Miss Masuda?" he boomed.

"Lose that big stinking cigar, mister, or go back to where you came from!" said my friend and colleague with steely authority in her voice.

Fowler stopped short, dumfounded, turned abruptly and rammed his cigar into a sand container in the hall.

He reentered the office slowly and with great care. He grinned apologetically.

"Sorry. I keep forgetting that it's not good form any more to smoke on somebody else's turf. But those things cost me six bucks apiece. Real Havana. Get 'em through Moscow. Don't ask me how. I'm Gene Fowler."

Reiko stood up and grasped Fowler's extended hand by the first two fingers, about as much as she could get a grip on.

"I am Reiko Masuda, assistant to Mr. Patrick Riordan, private investigator. And you are, if I am not mistaken, a business associate of Mr. Caravelli and Mr. Vanderhof. And the, ah, the *late* Mr. Levine." She drew herself up to look at least five-one in the presence of the overwhelming Mr. Fowler.

"Call me Gene, Reiko." He pronounced it "Reek-o", and she felt a small sting of anger.

"How can I help you, Mr. Fowler?"

"Well, Reek-o, Joe Caravelli told me you've been inquiring about his and my connection with Harry Levine, the conniving sonofabitch. Excuse me." Fowler blushed just slightly and fumbled with the gold buttons on his blazer.

"Yes, Mr. Fowler. I was present when Mr. Levine's body was discovered. I was the...technical advisor on the mystery weekend." She stretched for five-two, rising on her toes.

"Why sure! I remember you. You and that other little oriental gal were hangin' around at dinner. Kind of on the edge of things. Say, do you mind if I sit down?"

Reiko nodded at a chair in the corner and silently speculated on its ability to hold the bulk of Gene Fowler. He dragged it over to her desk and eased his ample rear onto the seat.

"I carry a lot of weight, honey, and it's burdensome. And after the events of the last few days, I'm real tired."

Fowler looked tired. As he sat there, Reiko began to realize that he wasn't as threatening as he had seemed to be. A man of his size is intimidating even if he has the soul of a pussycat.

He sighed, and squirmed on the chair. "Reek-o, Joe and me was brought into this bank deal by people we trusted. We didn't know Olin Vanderhof at first, but we had mutual friends. One of 'em was Barry Heathcote, God bless 'im, one of the sweetest guys who ever lived. We was all on the board together, Joe and Olin and Barry and me. And Harry Levine. Me and Joe *did* know Harry Levine, and we had no use for the bastard. Excuse me again. I can't think of Harry without some kind of bad language creepin' in."

"Don't mind me, goddammit," said Reiko, cheerfully.

Fowler shifted in his chair. "If we'd known that Levine was in the deal, we wouldn't have touched it. He is a genuine world-class...anal sphincter. You know what an anal sphincter is, honey?"

"Asshole," said Reiko with a blinding smile.

The big man cleared his throat and fished in his inside jacket pocket for a plastic wrapped cigar which he fondled nervously, fighting a craving to light it.

"Reek-o, there must be at least a dozen people in the Bay Area, and maybe six or eight folks around here who were absolutely delighted to hear that Harry was dead, most of 'em wishing they could've had the pleasure of sending him off, including Joe and me."

He stuck the wrapped cigar in his mouth and leaned forward. "But we didn't kill him."

At this point, my charming associate, the technical advisor, felt she was getting into dangerous water. Her confidence wavered for a moment. She made a quick decision.

"Do you suppose that you and Mr. Caravelli could meet with me and Mr. Riordan some time? Maybe tomorrow?"

"Sure, Reek-o. Joe can get down here in a couple of hours the way he drives. You let me know when and I'll fix it." The chair gave a sigh of relief as he rose from it.

"How about the other man? Mr. Heathcote?"

"Gosh, honey, I don't know where he is right now. He's been sick, I understand. Haven't seen him for months. Lives down the coast, you know. Sort of a loner."

"I'll call you when I talk to Mr. Riordan. Please give me your Carmel number." Reiko, a model of efficiency, shoved a note pad at Fowler and he scribbled the phone number. As he bent over, she thought she noticed that great head of hair shift slightly.

"Hell, all you got to do is dial the prefix plus FOWL. I conned 'em into that one, honey. You can get a lot of things if you got money. Aint' it a gas?"

The big man grabbed Reiko's hand in a grip that made her knuckles crack and made for the door, discarding his cigar wrapper and lighting the giant Havana with a Zippo in what seemed to be a single motion. He was happily puffing great gray clouds into the air as he reached the top of the stairs.

I had been sitting quietly listening to Reiko's story of her meeting with Fowler. She was describing the clouds of cigar smoke, dancing around with her hands high above her head.

"So, what do we do, love? You've got me committed to a meeting with these guys tomorrow. You think it'll be useful. OK, we'll meet. Make it nine-thirty. Here. Bring your samurai sword, kid. We'll get the truth out of 'em."

21

"Pat Riordan, meet Edgar Vanderhof."

Rᴇɪᴋᴏ ᴡᴇɴᴛ ᴛᴏ ʜᴇʀ ᴅᴇsᴋ to call Fowler, and I sat back in my chair and rested my feet on an open drawer. I needed a little quiet contemplation time. What's that they say about contemplating one's navel? I've never understood that. I don't think I've ever really looked at my navel very closely.

Something was nagging at me, something slight but hard to rationalize. A voice—a whispering voice—on the telephone had told me to go to the Carmel River Inn to find out something about Stewart Leonard. At he time of the call, Shirley Leonard was probably already dead. Why did the person call me? And who was he—or she? The caller wanted the body to be found—by me? He—or she, or it, or whatever—had probably called from the cottage moments after Shirley was killed. The caller was the killer.

But why was I picked to be the discoverer? Goddammit, how many people could know that I was connected to Shirley Leonard? That I was looking for Stewart?

I had accepted a missing person case for a pretty good fee. Now I was embroiled in two murders that were somehow connected. If I had only passed the bar exam in '56. I might now be a corporation lawyer, making fabulous money, golfing at the country club, sailing on my yacht. Oh, what the hell, I hate golf.

I reached for the phone to call Sally when it bleated in my hand.

"Hey, Riordan, did Emily Vanderhof come to see you?" Sally was calling *me*. Does that mean something. Should I marry her?

"You bet, sister." I did my inferior impression of the Bogart lisp. "The old broad was here and I think she's after my body."

"You stink, Pat. How could you talk like that about a lady of quality? What did you think, really?"

"Sally, you know me. You must know what I think. I am in love with Emily Vanderhof. She's a little older than I am. But then, I'm a little older than you are."

Sally whooped into the phone, causing me to jerk the receiver from my ear.

"You're twelve years older than I am and I admit to forty . . . something. How about dinner? We can talk. I'll pay. I owe you for Sunday."

"How about the Thai place on Cannery Row? You know it?"

"Great, Riordan. I'll see you there at six. Other phone's ringing. Bye."

I had never had Thai food before I found the little place tucked in a sort of loft on the Row. It was recommended to me by a dear friend to whom I shall refer as the World's Greatest Cartoonist (retired). This remarkable man created a popular comic strip just before World War II and kept it going single-handedly (with time out for his own military service) for more than forty years. He has lived in Carmel for many years and I treasure his friendship. I've always loved the funnies. But there's no art in cartoons any more. The new people are more interested in smartass jokes, politics and social commentary. The WGC (ret.) is an artist and a humorist.

But I mentioned Thai food. It's similar to other Asian foods in that a lot of it is stir-fried and some of it is spicy hot. That's an understatement. Some of it is *searing* hot. But the flavors (when not overcome by the spice) seem more subtle, somehow. I've grown to like it very much.

I arrived first that evening and was met, as usual, by the proprietor himself, a non-Asian who understands Thai cooking and the people who prepare it. The place was quiet, and I chose a seat on the banquette in a corner. When the waitress approached I ordered decaffeinated coffee. Coffee gets a special treatment here. You can hear it being ground just for your cup. The waitress, who looked like she had stepped out of a Singapore Airlines commercial, silently placed my coffee cup in front of me, and glided away. As you must know, I have this terrible weakness for small Asian women.

I had finished about half my coffee when I was aware of the fragrant presence of Sally Morse sliding in beside me. She kissed me on the cheek and immediately wiped the lipstick off with my napkin.

"I want you to meet somebody, Pat." Another person was there, looming over the little corner table. I looked up at a tall, thin man, about Sally's age, whose face was strangely familiar. He was smiling gently and extending his hand.

Achieving the standing position behind a small banquette table is very nearly impossible, but I tried. The salt and pepper shakers tumbled onto the floor, but I had presence enough to grab my coffee cup in my left hand. I stood in a half-crouch with a silly grin on my face. The tall man took my right hand, and steadied the table with his knees.

Sally spoke: "Pat Riordan, meet Edgar Vanderhof."

22

"Anson. That little weasel."

I HAD THESE HOT FLASHES, SEE? What, you say, only women in menopause have hot flashes? That's bullshit, mac. I got hot flashes, seeing Sally for the first time with a guy her own age. Was this a dumping ceremony and I the dumpee?

"Edgar just got in today from Los Angeles, Pat. His mother called him—about his father's problems. He's Olin's oldest son. We grew up together."

The hot flashes began to subside and I drew a normal breath. Edgar Vanderhof pulled up a chair and sat opposite Sally and me. He really looked like his father. I mean like Olin with twenty-five years or so peeled off. The lines in the face were not so deep, but they were the same lines.

"I didn't want to mess up your dinner date, but Sally was sure you wouldn't mind. Mother was not very informative on the phone. But I could tell she was disturbed. She's pretty cool most of the time."

Edgar *sounded* like his father. How often do the genes get arranged so precisely? He continued:

"Dad is a fine man. But I'm sure you realize that. And I'm sure you realize also that he is a bad businessman. Or unlucky, maybe. Or bad *and* unlucky. But he took care of us—I have three brothers— got us educated at good schools, and sent us off into the world equipped with professions and bank accounts."

"Edgar's a partner in a very important law firm," said Sally with a bright smile.

Anger welled up in me. Corporation lawyer, I'll bet. *I* could have been a big corporation lawyer with a three-piece suit and a fifty-dollar haircut, too, if I hadn't blown that bar exam because that dumb little Alice Engstrom had returned my ring that night before. . . . But that's another story.

Edgar's face was solemn. He ran long fingers through his thinning brown hair. The hair. That was the only thing that was different. Olin had a thick head of hair in his late sixties. Edgar's hair was in the process of departing. Aha! The genes of the mother. Baldness through the female. I made a mental note to look it up, and gently fingered the round bare spot on my crown.

"I never dreamed that my father could get himself in this deep. Oh, I knew he was. . .impractical. A dreamer, really. But such a basically loving man, such an intelligent man. . . ." Edgar's voice trailed off.

I remembered what George Spelvin had told me about how some of the Santa Clara faculty tried to recruit Olin for the Jesuits. Maybe that's what he was meant to be: a scholarly priest. If he had taken that route, there would have been no Edgar. We'da been better off, I thought, clamping my jaw.

"Mr. Riordan, my mother doesn't know the details. Just how bad is it?"

"All I know, Edgar, is what I got from Anson Ward, And it's *real* bad. It seems that if the bank goes under, your father and mother will be pretty close to broke."

"Anson. That little weasel. Hasn't he done enough?"

Edgar seemed to be staring into my coffee cup. Sally reached across the table for his hand. I had a small hot flash.

"You suspect Anson, Edgar?"

"Anson's not what he appears to be, Mr. Riordan. I'd better tell you. . . ."

I cut him off.

"I know about Anson. George Spelvin gave me the scoop on Anson. I've talked to him. He's not about to be voted Mr. Conge-niality, but I don't think he's misappropriated several million dollars."

Edgar sighed. "It could be a lot worse. My brothers and I are all doing very well. Our parents' home should be unencumbered. I can't believe Dad would mortgage that place. If worse came to worst, the four of us have more than enough to keep our parents comfortable. But Dad is proud—very, very proud."

"Have you talked with your father this trip, Edgar?"

"Oh, no. He doesn't know I'm here. That's the way mother wants it. And I think it's a good idea."

Edgar and Sally and I sat for a while in silence. Our pretty little Thai waitress approached discreetly, and Sally and I ordered. Edgar pleaded no appetite.

"What do you think, Mr. Riordan? I know you can only do so much...."

Sally interrupted: "The Vanderhofs are old friends of mine, Pat. And I know you can...." She was anxious.

She was also still holding Edgar's hand. I tried to stop grinding my teeth.

"Two things have to happen, folks, before we can pick up any momentum. We have to hear what the accountants learn about the condition of the bank. And we have to find out what's happened to Stewart Leonard." I finished my coffee and waggled a finger at the waitress for more.

"Reinhold and Freedman. Sid Freedman's an old family friend. His firm's probably doing the job. Maybe I can find out something." Edgar's face was gray and drawn. He looked suddenly older, even more like his father.

"You know what I'd like you to do, Edgar?" (I almost said, "Go back to LA." But I didn't.) "I'd like you to visit with your mom if you like and commiserate with her, but stay away from Olin...and, by all means, stay away from the bank."

He became a bit indignant. "Why Riordan? You think I can't help? You think I'd screw up?"

"No, sir. It's just that experience has taught me that you can't do a good investigative job if you're emotionally involved. No way. Leave it to me."

The food arrived and so did Reiko. She bounded into the dining room, wearing a shiny satin 49ers jacket and her Banana Republic hat pulled down over her ears.

She marched up to our table and, ignoring Sally and Edgar, announced in imperious fashion: "You got a call. At the office. I was there—*working*. You didn't tell me where you were going. I looked on your desk pad. And here you are." She tossed her head, triumphantly.

"I didn't write anything down."

"Oh, yes, you did. You wrote 'peanut butter sauce' in real small letters. So I knew I'd find you here. H'lo, Sally."

Sally, a little shaken, introduced Reiko to Edgar Vanderhof. My sterling assistant and caretaker softened up a little.

"My God, you look like your father," was all she could say.

"About the call, Reiko. Must have been pretty important to bring you over here." I like to get to the point. "Who was it?"

"Stewart Leonard. Calling from Big Sur. He left a number."

23

"I'd rather have hit Harry Levine, the bastard, and I'd have hit him a lot harder."

W ITH MISGIVINGS, I left Sally in the care of Edgar Vanderhof and went back to the office with Reiko. Our building is ten minutes away from Cannery Row on a quiet evening, and I hate to use public telephones. Almost without fail, when I try to use a public telephone, the mouthpiece has a rancid odor, or there is a hint that somebody has urinated nearby. Frequently there is a loud conversation within a few feet, or a convocation of motorcycles. I mourn the passing of the old fashioned phone booth. The smells were there,but you could get a reasonable amount of quiet.

I sat down at my desk, punched the numbers on the slip of paper Reiko handed me, and waited. Two rings, three rings, a voice, subdued and muffled:

"Hello."

"Stewart Leonard? Pat Riordan calling."

"Yes. . . I was almost sure. Nobody else would ask for me at this number."

"Where the hell have you been, Stewart? And why did you run off?"

"What is this, Riordan? I called your office because I read in the *Herald* that you found my sister's body. Where I've been is none of your damn business."

Well, it figured. How could Leonard know I was looking for him?

"Guess I'd better explain, Stewart. Olin Vanderhof is my client. When you went AWOL from his bank, he and a couple of other guys got sort of curious. They seemed to think it was, to say the least, *unusual* for the manager of a bank to leave town without even stopping the newspaper."

There was a long pause at the other end of the line.

"Can we get together, Riordan?"

"Hell, yes, Stewart. Name the time and the place."

"That's just it. I'm not ready to show in public—and there are good reasons. Any ideas?

I thought about it.

"You're driving, aren't you? Well, look, you're in Big Sur, right? A friend of mine lives in a canyon about halfway between you and Carmel. Come north, cross the Bixby Bridge, then over the Rocky Creek Bridge, then look for an opening in a clump of trees about a quarter of a mile past Rocky Creek on your right. If you get to Palo Colorado Road, you've come too far. Sound OK?"

"So far, OK."

"Back in the bushes, maybe fifty yards from the road, you'll find a ...well, a residence. Wait for me there."

"What time?"

I looked at my watch.

"In one hour, Stewart. Eight-thirty."

"I'll be there."

I pressed the disconnect and called Greg Farrell's number. It was Farrell's well-hidden cottage to which I had directed Leonard. There was no answer. I assumed that Greg was off on a camping trip, or giving a private lesson in Impressionist art to some impressionable young woman. It made no difference. Greg's method of locking up was to secure the hasp on the front door with a rusty teaspoon. There would be no problem.

Reiko had been sitting in my visitor's chair, slumped with her hands in her jacket pockets and her hat pulled down to her eyebrows.

"You are going to meet this guy at eight-thirty, in the black of night, at Greg's place, which you have trouble finding in broad daylight?"

"Man's gotta do what he's gotta do, Scarlett. The fact that Leonard is willing to come in out of the cold is enough to justify the effort."

"I'm going with you."

"You are *not* going with me."

"Overruled, Riordan. You need help on this one. I'm going."

Reiko stood up and walked to the door, turned to face me, folded her arms and planted her feet. Once, years ago, I asked another Japanese friend if he could tell me what "Reiko" meant.

"Depends on how it's written in Japanese. Closest I can come is 'spectacular girl-child.'" Nothing could be more appropriate.

My spectacular girl-child busied herself in closing down the office, locking the file cabinets, straightening her desk. Neither of us spoke as we walked down the stairs to Alvarado Street. The car was parked only a couple of spaces from the building entrance, and we got into it silently. Reiko gets angry if I try to open car doors for her. "You're stuck in the 50's mister. Get with it," she says.

Driving down Highway One at night has certain advantages. On the tight turns, you can see approaching headlights. The traffic is usually lighter than in the daytime. And, especially if you're on the ocean side, the dark is a blessing. You can't see the precipitous drops that make for clammy palms. You can't see the great scenery, either, and that's a minus. The road from Carmel to Morro Bay is one of the real California spectacles that everybody should experience at least once—in the daylight. It takes you across high, narrow bridges and along ledges carved out of the steep Santa Lucia range. It takes you through the Big Sur country, and past W.R. Hearst's "castle", a masterpiece of mixed architecture and a monument to excessive wealth and questionable taste. When the road curves inland at Morro Bay, it becomes pretty ordinary. But most of the trip you'll never forget.

I pointed the Mercedes out of Monterey on Pacific, winding up the hill to Highway One. Reiko slumped in her seat, staring out the window.

It wasn't until we were well past Carmel, near Yankee Point that she spoke, in a very small voice:

"You think there's any danger, Pat?"

"Na-a-ah. We are headed for the isolated residence of Greg Farrell, a place that most folks couldn't find without an inspired pack of bloodhounds. We're going to meet a guy who's been missing for a couple of weeks, and whom we've never seen. Maybe he's a criminal, maybe he's a CIA agent or a KGB spy or a middle eastern terrorist—or an undercover cop. Or all of the above."

"Be serious. I'm a little scared."

"Have no fear, little one," I said as I reached over and took her hand. "I took the precaution of bringing along my trusty blackthorn stick, secured in the boot."

The blackthorn walking stick, a thoughtful gift from my late wife, is the only weapon I own. Friends and colleagues have expressed grave concern that a mature man in my trade should refuse to arm himself. But I remain steadfast. For one thing, as I have said, I am a lousy marksman. For another, I have scrupulously avoided any case that could involve violent crime. This doesn't mean that I've been able to avoid danger altogether. I've found some dead bodies, more than my share. But it's like the old rhyme about the Purple Cow: "I'd rather see than be one."

So, if they get me (whoever "they" are), it'll be because I forgot to duck, rather than because I go unarmed. If I smell gunplay in a case, I call the cops.

It's very dark at eight o'clock in late November along Highway One. There's not much traffic, and you get the feeling that you're all alone on the edge of the world. When there's a fair sized moon on a clear night, it's exhilarating. But the moon wasn't with us as we passed Rocky Point, and Reiko and I began to strain our eyes for landmarks that indicated the turn-off to Greg's place.

It came up on us suddenly. A clump of trees on the left. I slowed down just in time to turn into a rutted dirt driveway that twisted around through some tall weeds to a clearing about twenty yards in front of the cottage.

I pulled the Mercedes up behind an unwashed Mercury sedan. Reiko and I sat for a few moments with the headlights on. There was nobody in the Merc. There wasn't a sound except the low rumble of my exhaust. I made a mental note to get the muffler checked.

"Stay here, my friend," I said.

"You're going to leave me here?" asked Reiko.

"Stay. Lock the doors when I get out. Give me the flashlight out of the glove compartment."

I cut the engine and turned off the lights. It was like being in a darkroom at first. Then, when my eyes adjusted, I could see the stars and the outline of the horizon. I plunged into the brush in the direction of Greg's cottage.

When I got within twenty feet of the house, I heard a small sound in the silent night. From my right, a shadowy figure uncoiled and planted a large angry fist in my face. I hit the ground like a sack of manure.

"Hey!" was all I could manage as I felt a warm trickle of blood from my nose. I lay on my back, flashlight clutched in my hand, its beam uncontrolled.

A voice came from behind me, stern but a little shrill:

"Leave him alone, you sonofabitch, or I'll split your head open with this stick." I rolled my eyes back and my flashlight picked up Reiko waving my blackthorn weapon like a big league hitter anticipating an inside pitch. I aimed the flash ahead and upward to see a slender black man looking angry and surprised at the same time.

"You're Riordan," he said, an allegation I couldn't really deny. "You got my sister killed, you bastard."

At that moment my nose hurt a great deal, and I was not going to question the illogic that led Stewart Leonard to that conclusion.

"Stewart, you hit me with a world class sucker punch out of the dark. Let's go inside the house and get a good look at each other. And mind what the little lady says or, by golly, she'll break your skull."

I prayed briefly that Greg Farrell had paid his light bill, removed the rusty teaspoon from the hasp, and opened the door. Gesturing Leonard and Reiko to enter ahead of me, I fumbled for the light switch. All three of us flinched when the bright naked bulbs came on. Reiko was still poised to deliver a whistling line drive with my blackthorn stick.

Stewart Leonard was about my height, just under six feet, but weighed maybe twenty pounds less than I do. He was a handsome man, a male version of his beautiful sister, and I would have known him anywhere after seeing Shirley. He wore an expensively tailored three-piece suit that was badly in need of cleaning and pressing, and his soiled shirt was open at the throat. He looked rather like he'd been on a week's drunk. He was still angry.

"Shirley was a high class tramp, I guess, but she was my sister. She may have made a living on her back—but she was incapable of harming anybody. When I read that she'd been found dead in a motel room by some cheap private eye, I figured you had something to do with it."

I had grabbed a dishtowel from a rack over the sink and was wiping the blood from my nose. Reiko was standing by, blackthorn at the ready, eager to spring to my aid if need be.

"Stewart, I am not cheap. Vanderhof has to pay me five thousand dollars for finding you. And that's what it's all about—finding you. Your sister was looking for you, too. She got to me through Vanderhof. I liked her. I sure as hell didn't kill her, and I don't know who did. But I think it must have been the same person who killed Harry Levine."

Leonard lowered himself onto one of Greg's two kitchen chairs. He closed his eyes and sighed. He pulled a soiled handkerchief from his breast pocket and wiped his face, although it was too cool in the house for a sweat. He looked up at me. I pressed the dishtowel hard against the septum.

"I'm sorry, Riordan. I've been angry for a while and you got some of it you didn't deserve. I'd rather have hit Harry Levine, the bastard, and I'd have hit him a lot harder. The only pleasant moment I've had in a couple of weeks was when I heard somebody got Harry. I wish I knew who. The guy deserves a medal."

"At first I had a notion that you did it, Stewart. You were AWOL at he bank. But I didn't think you'd kill Shirley. Then I thought you were probably floating in the Bay."

Reiko at last lowered her weapon and sat quietly on her heels on the floor. I soaked the dish towel in cold water from the kitchen tap and pressed it to my nose. I didn't think it was broken, but it hurt like hell.

Leonard appeared to relax. He sat in the straight chair with his hands in his lap and began to talk, quietly and reflectively:

"The Farmers' and Ranchers' Bank was going to be my spring-board to the big stuff. I'm the toughest kind of yuppie, Riordan, a black yuppie. I had done well in Cincinnati. It's a good town. It's my *home* town. But California—and the chance to build a bank of my own—ah, that was what I had been looking for. A new life, a new world, a real step up."

Stewart's eyes lit up for a couple of seconds, but his face suggested sadness in repose.

"Riordan, do you have any notion how tough it is for a black man in the banking business to rise above a certain level? Inner city branches are fine. You deal with your own. Ever notice in some of those McDonald's TV commercials that when they're black, they're *all* black. Everybody in the place is black, the cooks, the wait-resses, the customers. Well, I wanted more, and this job in Hollister seemed to be the way out. I'd stay a few years, build up the bank, and move on to San Francisco or LA.

"It was mean in the early days. Most of the directors, maybe even Vanderhof, didn't know when they sent for me that I was a black man. When I got here, my record and my references were so good, they couldn't find any reason to turn me down. They smiled and said, 'The job is yours, Mr. Leonard—but you must prove yourself.'

"Those old farm boys and ranchers in San Benito County, they're very tough. They weren't altogether sure they'd be comfortable coming to a black banker for crop loans. But I won 'em over, Riordan. I worked my ass off. I drove all over the county and paid a call on about every damn one of 'em. And in a year and a half, two years, they were all callin' me 'Stew'. Didn't have me home to dinner, but they trusted me in the business relationship. And that little bank did well from the first year on, until...."

Leonard had been fidgeting in his chair. He stood up and went to a window to stare out into the dark.

"Early in my time at the bank, I bought a computer and set it up in my bedroom in Carmel. With it and a modem and the entry codes into the bank's computer, I could monitor all transactions and call up records from home. I didn't want anything to go wrong.

"On the third of this month, I was checking some things out and came across some very heavy loans that I couldn't remember approving to an outfit in San Francisco called Sterling Ventures. These were big numbers, Riordan, secured by Carmel Valley property. I made a check of all the business involving Sterling Ventures. There was a lot if stuff. Loans to the outfit in late summer—almost six million dollars. I panicked. Somebody has been bypassing me.

"When I went into the bank the next day, I dug out all the information. The deal got flakier and flakier. I drove out to see one of the properties that was supposed to be security. Hell, it turned out to be a country club I *belong* to, a goddam golf course. I'm on the board. Never heard of Sterling Ventures. How do you like that?"

Leonard couldn't know of my passionate dislike for golf. I nodded and murmured a sympathetic but unintelligible murmur. He went on:

"I told my people I had to go to San Francisco on business. When I got to the address listed for Sterling Ventures, there was an empty office. Not even a secretary. Just a firm name in gold on the locked door. A dummy, a goddam dummy. When I made a few inquiries, I found the office had been rented by a man who said he was the president of Sterling Ventures. Guess who, Riordan? Harry M. Levine."

24

"You guys would like some tea, wouldn't you?"

*T*HE TROUBLE WITH HARRY. It's an old Hitchcock movie about a dead body that causes all kinds of problems in an otherwise peaceful little town. It was in the mid-fifties, I think, with a young Shirley MacLaine before she discovered that she had been several other people over a considerable period of time.

Our own trouble with Harry was growing more complicated. Harry was dead. Harry was—to say the least—unpopular. Harry was, according to report, a real shit. Somebody killed him and nobody was shedding any tears.

I thought for a moment about what Stew Leonard had just told me.

"Did you pursue it further, Stewart? Did you try to find out anything else about Sterling Ventures?"

"No, Riordan. When I found out that Harry *was* Sterling Ventures, I came on back. I had to think the thing through. I knew Harry pretty well. He'd been on the bank's board since the beginning, and I had sat in many a meeting with him. We'd drunk together and eaten together. He was the kind of a guy you had to get to know really well in order to hate. He was cruel, crude and bigoted. He made a big show of accepting me, but took every opportunity to get a little nasty innuendo into the conversation. He'd tell the worst kind of racist jokes. But then he'd say, 'Oh, not like *you*, Stew. The folks I'm talkin' about were just out of the

115

cotton fields.' You know what I mean, Riordan?"

I nodded slowly. "Yeah, Stew, all you guys can tap dance and slam dunk and throw the javelin. I know what you mean."

"So I hated him just because he was Harry Levine. Then when I found out he was Sterling Ventures, and was into the bank for almost six million dollars, I got very sick. I was so sure I had everything covered."

He was passing his soiled handkerchief from hand to hand, occasionally dabbing his face. He looked like a man in great pain.

Reiko stood up, placed my blackthorn stick reverently on a counter top, and picked up a battered teakettle from Greg's propane stove. She began examining the contents of jars and canisters scattered around the kitchen.

"He's gotta have some teabags. You guys would like some tea, wouldn't you? It's cold as a well-digger's ass in here."

She was right. It was cold. There was a wind coming from the ocean, and Greg's cottage was porous. The heating system was an ancient pot-bellied stove, but I couldn't see firing it up for the short time we were likely to be there.

"Cup o' tea'd be great for me, love. Stew?"

He nodded, and a faint smile erased part of the anger from his face.

"Stewart, were you gone from the bank for any length of time—in the past year?"

"Well, yes. I had four weeks coming. I took one in the spring—April, I think—and then three weeks the latter part of August, running through Labor Day week."

"Late summer. Those troublesome loans were made in late summer, you said. Has that occurred to you?"

His eyes widened and his jaw dropped a half inch.

"You know, I didn't even think of that. I was so shook up about *finding* the loans. How goddam stupid can you get? It must have happened that way. They did it when I was gone."

"They? Who could approve loans of that size—besides you?"

"We had it set up that any member of the board could. I have—or had—an assistant, Frances Engel. She could do it, too. She had my power of attorney. She's very competent. I've known her a long time. She's handled a lot of major loans. But she wouldn't touch anything in seven figures—without authority from a board member. In my absence that would usually be Olin Vanderhof—or Barry Heathcote. Barry was usually around. That is, until the last six months. I guess I haven't seen Barry for quite a while. Somebody told me he was ill."

"When you found the records of these loans on your computer, didn't it indicate who approved them?"

"No. Should have been there. It'd be on the loan documents themselves. They should be in the vault."

Reiko brought the tea in three dissimilar cups. It was hot, all right, but lacked something.

"There was only one bag," she said, reading my mind. "I did the best I could. You're going to have to get inside the bank aren't you?"

What I had been thinking was that we were going to have to get inside the Farmers' and Ranchers' Bank of San Benito County. We were going to have to look at those records without asking the board of directors for permission. I felt a pang of conscience. I hated to think of doing anything behind Olin Vanderhof's back. But, what the hell.

"Stewart, do you have your keys to the bank with you? And can you get around the security system?"

He was on his feet immediately. "Sure, Riordan. You mean to go there *tonight?*"

"No better time. Two people have been killed. We don't want any more fatalities if we can help it. Reiko, we'll take Stew's car and you can drive yourself home in mine."

"Negative, Riordan. I'm still the chief investigator on the Harry Levine murder. I'm the *technical advisor.*"

So, off we went towards Hollister, Leonard and I in his Mercury, Reiko following grimly in my Mercedes.

I don't think either Stewart or I said a word all the way to the bank. Well, that's not quite right. I remember once glancing into the rear-view mirror and seeing the Mercedes close behind. I think my words were, "Goddammit, she's following too close!" But Stew didn't seem to notice.

When we got to Hollister, we parked on a side street a good block from the bank. By that time it was nearly eleven, and there was little traffic on the main street leading into the city and not a soul on foot as far as we could see.

Reiko and I stood in the shadows while Stewart went around the back of the building to some secret device through which he could deactivate the alarm system.

Seconds later, we all slipped through the front door. Stewart led us silently to his office. He closed the door and turned on the lights. "No windows here. Cheaper to air-condition with no windows." He looked wistful. "Hell, I like windows."

"So what happens now, Stewart?" I said, just a wee bit annoyed.

"Our loan files are in the vault. It's big and it's fireproof, but it was cheap. Our board didn't think we'd need an elaborate time lock or any of the other security innovations of modern banking. So they went second class. All it takes is the combination. I've got a flashlight in my closet. We'd better not turn on the lights in the lobby."

He produced an aluminum flashlight about two feet long and, after carefully turning out the lights in his office, went out into the bank proper. He led the way to the vault, and after a few deft twists of the dial, swung open the great door.

"For God's sake, don't close the door behind you. There's supposed to be a way to get out if the door is accidentally closed, but I've never tried it. No use taking chances."

Leonard pointed the flash at a row of file cabinets deep in the vault beyond the safe deposit boxes.

When we reached the files, he scanned the framed labels and flicked a small key from a heavy bunch he carried. In a moment the drawer was open, and he was holding the flashlight high with his left hand and searching feverishly through the file folders with his right. He looked from front to back, than back to front. Angrily, he hit the file drawer with the heel of his hand and said in a very loud voice, "They're gone, Riordan, they're all gone. Somebody got here first."

25

There were sounds of battle in my dreams.

Reiko and I went out to the cars while Leonard stayed behind to secure the bank.

"Wild goose chase, Riordan. Your boy Leonard is pretty uptight, isn't he? Are you sure he's all that he seems to be?" She looked at me with that narrow-eyed sideways glance that she uses so effectively. What it says is, "I'm not that easy to con, mister."

"What do you mean, Reiko? You don't buy his story?"

"It's just a little hard for me to believe that if this guy is as good as he says he is and Vanderhof thinks he is, he could have let six million dollars in loans get away from the bank without noticing the money going bye-bye."

"He was out of town, Reiko-san. On vacation."

"Riordan, when the guy first told us he discovered the business with Sterling Ventures on his computer, he said he went into the bank the next day and checked out the whole account. Wouldn't that mean he looked at the paper work then?"

She was right. Stewart Leonard *had* been back to the bank. He could easily have dug out all the information on the questionable loans without arousing any suspicion. Why in hell did he drag us over here late at night when he knew what was in the files? Was he going through the motions?

At that moment, Leonard arrived, swinging a bunch of keys that must have weighed three-quarters of a pound. He seemed more relaxed. He was humming what sounded like an aria from *La Boheme*.

"I'll take my car back to Big Sur, Riordan. I don't think it's wise for me to appear in public just yet. I think whoever killed Levine and my sister would probably want to get rid of me."

"You're running again, Stew. Why did you run in the first place?"

He looked straight at me with a mirthless grin.

"Six million bucks in bad loans to a dummy corporation. *Six mill* out of the bank run by a *black man*, Riordan. Are you too white bread to see the problem, man? There's folks in San Benito County who just wouldn't understand."

I started to ask him about the contradiction that Reiko had pointed out, but decided against it. Maybe just a little more rope. . . .

"Where are you staying, Stew? In case I need to get hold of you."

"You've got my phone number, Riordan. I'll be there most of the time. You'd never find the place, anyhow. It's just a cabin on a hilltop I bought three years ago to use on weekends. Nobody knows about it. Call me if you hear anything."

He slid in behind the wheel of the Mercury and drove off into the night.

I couldn't help wondering if I had been taken. Reiko was right. The guy had told us conflicting stories. He might not be as squeaky clean as he seemed to be.

It was after midnight when we left Hollister. The night was clear and the stars were bright. The stars were bright, but I wasn't so sure about me. Reiko sat beside me with her eyes closed and pretended to sleep.

When I pulled up in front of her building, she gave me a peck on the cheek and bounced out of the car.

"Fowler and Caravello. Nine-thirty at the office. Be ready."

I watched her run up the short flight of stairs into the building. Then I headed down Lighthouse on my way back to Carmel.

When I turned right on Forest up the hill towards the Holman Highway, I noticed that a pair of headlights I had been aware of shortly after I left Reiko's place had turned with me and kept pace at a distance of half a block. The guy in the other car and I might have been the only two people awake in Pacific Grove at one-thirty in the morning.

I didn't think much about the other car at first. When I'm driving in familiar territory, I often get lost in my own thoughts and am saved from destruction by a sort of automatic pilot that knows every street on the Peninsula of Monterey.

Forest turns into the Holman Highway at a point on the hill where the Army has erected some new barracks on government property that must offer the most spectacular views to service people south of the Presidio of San Francisco. God, what a spot, I thought, remembering my basic training days on the sand dunes of Fort Ord in '52.

The other car was still behind me, maybe a hundred yards, still keeping pace. I was on the downhill run past the Community Hospital and the fire station, bearing right on the feeder to Highway One. I headed up Carmel Hill.

As soon as I got on the main road, the car behind me put on a burst of speed and swung to the inside lane. He was running alongside me in a matter of seconds. And when I glanced to my left, I could see the driver leaning in my direction with his arm out-stretched. At first, I thought he was signalling me, as somebody might let you know you're getting a flat tire or your tail light's out. But then I saw a tiny flash of light from the end of the driver's arm and simultaneously heard a pop on my window, and I knew I'd been shot at.

We were almost at the Carpenter Street light. I gunned the Mercedes off the highway down Carpenter, hoping that I could attract the attention of the Carmel police. But when I looked back, the car was gone. It had stayed on Highway One.

I guess I was hyperventilating some as I drove down the truck route all the way to Junipero. I had made a panicky wrong turn and there was nothing to do but go on down to Sixth and up the hill again. The Mercedes automatically turned in the driveway and stopped. My hands automatically switched off the lights and turned the ignition key. I got out, pretty weak in the knees. It is not, my friends, that I have never heard the whine of bullets near my ears. But enemy gunfire is a good deal different from a shot in the dark.

It was three a.m. before sheer exhaustion caught up with me and I slept, fitfully. There were sounds of battle in my dreams. I thought I'd shaken those long ago.

26

Frances Engel demurely crossed her legs.

H EY, RIORDAN, it's eight o'clock." Reiko's voice was clear in my ear, and I didn't remember picking up the phone. The words registered, but their meaning took some time to penetrate. I had a headache, my nose was glued to my pillow with blood from Stew Leonard's sucker punch, and my head seemed to be full of mashed potatoes.

"Did you hear me?" The voice persisted. "Those two clowns will be here at nine-thirty, remember? Fowler and Caravelli? Get your old butt out of bed."

If this little woman were my wife, I thought, I could whisper an obscenity and roll over. I did not want to get up. I wanted to stay in bed all day.

Then, abruptly, the shock of the night returned. I saw the tiny spit flame, and heard the bullet hit the glass of the car window on the driver's side, felt the panic of the living target.

"Reiko-san, listen to me. Somebody followed me from your place last night and took a shot at me. Somebody knows where you live and staked you out. Then he followed me until I was out on Highway One, and took a shot at me. And it was close."

She was quiet for a moment.

"How close?"

"I don't really know. Close. I just got out of the car and ran into the house. People don't shoot at me very often. And it sort of upsets me when they. do. This person must think I know more than I do. And he, she or it knows where you live. *You've* got to be careful, little one."

"*You* be careful, Riordan. I can't...run this place without you. But you better wash your face and come on over here. Those guys will be here in about ninety minutes."

I hung up the phone and got out of bed. It was cold in my bedroom. No matter how much you remodel these old Comstock houses from the twenties, there are still problems. My place was meant to be heated primarily by a massive stone fireplace downstairs. Nowadays, people who live in these quaint Carmel houses use little electric room heaters when it's really cold. I jumped into a heavy jogging suit I wear around town. I never jog. It gets me in the knees. But I walk along and wave at people who do jog. They probably think I'm a retired marathoner who has just slowed down for a breather.

I went outside to look at my wounded Mercedes.

The car was covered with moisture, as if it had been left out in a heavy rain. The dew drenches everything in the morning on this part of the California coast. In the window on the driver's side, near the upper left corner, was a small neat hole, surrounded by a spider-webby pattern of stress-fracture in the glass. The bullet must have passed about three inches from my nose. I found the impact on the right door frame and the flattened slug on the floor. It looked like a .22, about the right size for the holes in the heads of Harry Levine and Shirley Leonard.

After a shower, I felt a little more alive, despite the fact that I had to mop the bathroom floor and wipe off the toilet seat. When the bathroom window's closed, the water has to go somewhere. I made another of my useless mental notes to do something about the shower. A lot of my mental notes get erased. Short-term memory loss is a sign of...aw, hell, I forget.

I got to the office before our guests arrived. Reiko got up from her desk and hugged me, something she never does unless she is distraught or it's my birthday.

"Pat, maybe we ought to just dump this case. It's getting a little too rough. And I think you ought to protect yourself. So I borrowed this from my uncle."

From her top drawer she gingerly produced a small nickel-plated revolver, which she extended to me by gripping the barrel in her fist.

I took the gun by the butt with two fingers and flipped out the chamber. It was loaded and the safety was off. I shook the bullets out into my left hand.

I spoke very softly: "Reiko-san, I want you to wrap these little bullets in some tissues, and take them and the gun back to Shiro. If I had taken it from you by grasping the butt in my hand and putting my finger through the trigger guard as you handed it to me just now, it might have gone off and killed you. As for last night, I couldn't have protected myself with a Browning Automatic Rifle or a Garand M-1, both of which I handled with reasonable proficiency many years ago. I am not playing cops and robbers or bang! you're dead. That's for the police. *Wakarumasu ka?*" A hell of an opportunity to use my Toshiro Mifune Japanese from *Shogun*.

"*Wakarimasu*, Riordan-san," she said, putting the hardware back in the drawer.

I had just sat down in my chair when our guests appeared at the door.

Fowler, the big man, had been well described to me by Reiko. He was, if anything, bigger than I had imagined. And he *was* wearing somebody else's hair.

In contrast, Joe Caravelli was small and thin with a full black mustache. He reminded me of somebody who used to play for the Oakland A's back in their championship seasons in the 70's.

With the men was a woman, a dark-haired, bland-looking type wearing large black-rimmed glasses. She wore a business-like tailored suit and sensible shoes, but somehow I got the impression that she was one of those women who would whip off her glasses and let down her hair and turn into early Ava Gardner. Her figure, as my practiced eye could perceive it, was promising, and her calves were nicely curved. I don't know why I'm preoccupied with calves. She was introduced as Frances Engel, assistant to the manager of the Farmers' and Ranchers' Bank.

I sent Reiko to borrow a couple of chairs from the accountant's office next door. There's a young fellow in that office who's been

mooning over her ever since we moved in, and he'd jump off the
building if she'd ask. Sure enough, he came puffing in with two
chairs and ducked out with a shy smile. Nice kid, I thought, but he'll
never get past mama-san.

The three visitors sat and looked at me, and I looked back with a
genial smile. Reiko dragged her desk chair into the room.

"Well, folks, what are we going to talk about?" I asked, sweetly.
Somebody had to start.

Fowler, who dominated the room with his bulk, put the ball in
play.

"I guess you know most of what we know, Riordan. Joe and me,
we're board members at that bank. So was Harry Levine. Levine's
dead, but that's not so bad. I think he was a crook, anyhow. Olin
Vanderhof's accountants are in the process of checking out the
bank's records. Stew Leonard's disappeared. Me and Joe have got a
lot of money tied up in this bank thing, Riordan. And the two of us
and our *real* wives were in that bunch at the hotel when Levine got
shot."

Joe Caravelli pulled at his mustache and said nothing. Frances
Engel demurely crossed her legs. I notice things like that. Fowler
went on:

"If word gets out that there's something strange going on at our
bank, we're sunk, man. Joe's gonna lose his ass, and so am I."

I looked at Caravelli.

"Anything to add?" I asked.

Caravelli had a dry, reedy voice: "We're business men, Mr.
Riordan. About the only thing we have in common is our acquaintance with Olin Vanderhof and our involvement with the bank.
Gene and I are members at Cypress Point, and we met Olin through
mutual friends. We played some golf together. Every now and then,
Harry Levine would play to make a foursome. Then when Olin got
this bank idea, we all took a piece of it. And Stew Leonard seemed to
be the right man to run the show. But...."

Miss Engel re-crossed her legs, diverting my attention for but a
fraction of a second.

"How did you guys feel about Stew's being black?"

Fowler reacted: "Hey, man, he had nothing but the best

credentials. We got no prejudice, do we, Joe? This is California, amigo. Home of the Rainbow Coalition."

I ignored Fowler's bit of misinformation, and turned my attention to Miss Engel.

"And how did you feel about working for a black man?"

She looked at me through those great round spectacles that magnified just slightly a pair of well made-up brown eyes.

"It was a business relationship, Mr. Riordan. I have nothing but the greatest respect for Stewart Leonard."

I tossed the next question at all three of them: "Who is Barry Heathcote?"

There was surprise on their faces.

"Why do you ask that?" Caravelli was the first to speak.

"The name popped up over in Hollister when I was snooping around. Who is he?"

Frances Engel took charge. That's what would worry me about Miss Engel, despite her handsome calves. She would try to lead on the dance floor, and in bed, she'd...well, you know.

"Mr. Heathcote is a stockholder in our bank, a member of our board of directors, and a well-respected citizen of Monterey County. Unfortunately, he has been ill for an extended period, and has not attended meetings for nearly a year. He has an impeccable background: a retired manufacturer from the East. A widower. A quiet man."

"Anybody ever visit him?" I asked.

"Frankly, none of us knows him that well," said Caravelli. "He's more of a friend of Olin's."

"Hell," said Fowler, "I'm sure I saw his picture in the paper no more'n a couple of months ago. Didn't look sick. Some guys just don't like meetings."

Sam Pearcy, the more or less retired Hollister insurance man, had told me that he'd known Heathcote a long time. Something didn't quite fit. I looked at Fowler.

"Are you *sure* you saw Heathcote's picture?"

"Well, it sure as hell looked like him. But those guys in the society pages of the *Pine Cone* all look alike: white hair, expensive clothes and highball glasses. All alike. Maybe I just *thought* it was

Heathcote."

At this point the office phone rang, and Reiko slipped quietly into the front office to answer it.

Miss Engel was leaning forward.

"Mr. Riordan, I need to tell you that certain loans were made late in the summer that I have only now become aware of. They are . . . suspicious, to say the least."

"To Sterling Ventures?"

She looked shocked. "Yes, Sterling Ventures. How did you . . .?"

"It's Balestreri, Pat." Reiko's voice was a shade too loud, and it carried a note of alarm.

"Excuse me, folks," I said to my guests, as I picked up the phone. "Yeah, Tony, what's up?"

"We got a report from a tourist, Pat. Seems he was parked on one of the view turnouts overlooking the Bixby Bridge, and thought he saw a man sleeping way down at the base. We checked it out. Man was dead, Pat. Black, about forty, well dressed. Drivers license says he's Stewart Leonard. Business card says he's manager of a bank over in Hollister. Ring any bells?"

27

Take one or two .22 slugs in the back of the head and don't call me in the morning.

WHEN I DROPPED THAT BOMB on the people in my office, there was genuine astonishment. As I think about it now, I'm not sure that Fowler, Caravelli and Engel were surprised that Stewart had been found dead, or surprised that the body was under the bridge. There had always been a suspicion of foul play in connection with Stewart's disappearance. But my guests probably would have better been able to accept Stewart's death if he'd been found shot in a hotel room like his sister and Harry Levine. So much more civilized. Somebody found deceased at the base of the Bixby Bridge had either to have jumped or been pushed. Or maybe just dispatched and dumped. At that moment, we didn't know.

I told Balestreri I'd meet him at the county morgue in Salinas, and promised the others that we'd continue our discussion at a later date.

Reiko was already on the phone to Vanderhof's office on another line. She called to me to take the call on hold when I hung up. When I picked up the receiver and punched the button, I heard the unctuous voice of Anson Ward, apparently talking to his employer: "...dead under the bridge, from the fall I should imagine."

I spoke: "Anson, put Mr. Vanderhof on."

The gentle voice of Olin Vanderhof came on the line. "Anson

has just told me that Stewart Leonard is dead. Is this true, Mr. Riordan?"

"I'm afraid so. A friend in the sheriff's office just called me. They found a body under the Bixby Bridge. The ID he carried was certainly Stewart's. I'm going over to Salinas to check it out."

There was a pause. "I'm not quite sure how you're going to be able to identify Stewart, Mr. Riordan. Unless, of course, you've seen him alive recently. However, I'm not going to ask you about that. If the body in the morgue is indeed that of Stewart Leonard, our business then is finished. If and when you confirm the identity, I'll have Anson send you a check."

There was very little to suggest genuine concern in Vanderhof's manner. It was simply as though a business deal had been concluded, and he was affirming the contract.

"I'll call you as soon as I know anything for sure, Mr. Vanderhof." I wondered why I was always being so formal with this man. He wasn't *that* much older than me. And it made me pretty uncomfortable to know that Vanderhof suspected that I had met with the living Stewart Leonard without reporting the fact to him.

I met Balestreri in the front office of the morgue. He greeted me with a clout on the shoulder that made me stumble.

"So, here's your mysterious missing man, Riordan. This *is* the guy, isn't it? And it's like I said, isn't it? Out of the bank with a bundle and off to the races. Or did he just get mixed up with the wrong crowd?"

"Let's make sure, Sergeant. Let's confirm the ID."

Balestreri led me back to the cold storage drawers and pulled one out. The face he uncovered was Stew Leonard's, looking even more like his sister in death.

"Yeah. It's Leonard."

We walked back to the office. Balestreri was whistling "It's a Small World", an inane little tune that was totally inappropriate at the time.

"Was it the fall from the bridge?" I asked, as we both sat down on a large leather couch.

Balestreri pursed his lips. "Oh, that would have done it, all right. Strange you should ask. That's a hell of a long way down. But in this case, completely unnecessary. He's got a bullet hole in his head. One shot at the base of the brain, small caliber. What does that suggest to you, Riordan?"

"Professional work, maybe? An execution? By somebody's order?"

Take one or two .22 slugs in the back of the head and *don't* call me in the morning. The people who follow the profession of killing are neat and efficient. But, somehow, I couldn't conceive of a professional job on Leonard. A neat job, yes, but not professional. According to the coroner's report, Leonard was dead for between one and two hours before he got broken up on the rocks at the base of the bridge.

I thanked Balestreri and started back to Monterey. I had not expected this turn of events. My reading up to that time was that Stew Leonard was somehow directly involved in the suspicious financial dealings with Sterling Ventures, and a pretty good suspect in the murder of Harry Levine. I was sure, though, that he had not murdered his sister. He had seemed genuinely disturbed at her death. And now somebody had disposed of Stew.

When I got back to the office, Reiko was gone. It was near noon, and I assumed she had run out for lunch with one of her cronies in the building.

I called Sally.

"Morse Travel, may I help you?"

"Come over here and sit on my lap. I need sympathy."

"I'll be damned if I'll come over there. It's lunch time. Meet me at the Thunderbird."

The Thunderbird is actually a large book store in a complex call the Barnyard just off Highway One south of Carmel at the entrance to Carmel Valley. It's a great place to go when the summer tourist season is over. You can browse and you can sip coffee for a couple of hours and nobody will bother you. And you can have lunch. Great soup. The place is ruled with a disciplined hand by a lady of my acquaintance. She brooks no nonsense, and she knows how to make a buck in the book trade.

Sally was sitting at a small table in a remote corner of the dining room when I got there.

"How's Edgar?" I asked with a cheery smile.

"You are a bastard, Riordan. Edgar Vanderhof is a childhood chum. As a kid he was kind of a wimp, and never once invited me behind the barn to show me his whistle. Now he's a grown-up married wimp who's losing his hair. But he's a friend. What's bothering you?"

I told her about Stew Leonard.

"I am back to the old drawing board, or square one, whichever cliche you prefer, Sally. Olin hired me to find Leonard. Leonard's dead. And now Olin wants to pay me off. But I'm not through with this case. I want to know what it's all about. And I'm not sure I can trust any of the people involved."

Sally can be just about any kind of woman you could imagine. She's been around the block a few times. She married a very persuasive young musician when they were still in college. Being a good-hearted soul, she went along with his dreams of jazz immortality in the sixties, and hung in there until it was obvious that there was no hope for the guy to make it to the top. Yet, I've never heard her refer to her ex-husband with great bitterness. Strongest word she uses is "bum." Sometimes "sweet, well-meaning bum." She's a compassionate woman with a strong will and a taste for *haute couture*. A lot like the woman I lost in an auto crash more than ten years ago.

She looked grave at this moment.

"Pat, I wish I could help. I don't see how I can, but I wish I could. I can soothe your fevered brow a little. Or take you home and put us both to bed. But it won't help your problem. Forget about Edgar Vanderhof. Forget about the whole family. It's a police matter now. God knows it's all bound to come out. The missing bank manager, the hooker, the hotshot from the City. Some good reporter is going to put 'em all together."

"Ever hear of Barry Heathcote?"

"Sure. Why?"

"What do you know?"

"Rich. Society guy. Never used my agency, damn him. Came out here from somewhere on the East Coast. Retired. Lives down Big Sur way in a humungous house. Saw him last summer at one of the

Bach Festival concerts."

"Had you heard he was in poor health?"

"No. He must be getting on in years, though. Never can tell. Why Heathcote, Pat?"

"A hunch. Keeps coming back. He's on the board at Vanderhof's bank. Probably nothing to it, but...."

Sally looked at me curiously. Then she leaned toward me and kissed me on the lips. I suddenly felt relieved and almost calm. I returned the kiss with unseemly ardor for a restaurant *tete a tete* at the lunch hour.

"Thank you, ma'am, you've been lots of help. Hold the good thoughts. Have a nice bowl of soup. I've got to follow another hunch."

I kissed her again noisily and left, calling across the room that I would phone her later.

28

Nobility is a terrible burden to bear.

I CAUGHT TONY BALESTRERI at the sheriff's substation on Agua-jito Road, grabbed him by the arm and dragged him into a corner.

"Was there a car? Anywhere? A blue Mercury sedan?"

"No way, Pat. Just the body. Why?"

"We were in Hollister last night. At the bank. When we split up, Leonard said he was going back down to Big Sur. What happened to the car?"

Leonard must have gone somewhere else when he left Reiko and me after our unsuccessful tour of the Farmers' and Ranchers' Bank. But where would he go at that hour? I knew that if I could find out, the whole thing would unravel.

"Pat, he was hauled from someplace else, probably dead, at least dying, and pushed or thrown over the rail at the south end of the bridge. If he left you in a car, it was dropped somewhere. If it was registered to him, I can put out an inquiry about it. See if it turns up."

"Please do so, Tony. The guy went to see somebody when he left me. I don't know why or who, but answers to those questions can solve my whole problem...maybe."

When I got back to my office, Anson Ward was waiting for me. He was sitting on a corner of Reiko's desk, watching her preside grimly over her computer keyboard, pressing keys and combinations of keys with great deliberation.

Anson turned as I entered and smiled his oily smile.
"Your little girl here, Mr. Riordan, is truly a virtuoso at the keyboard. She's genuinely gifted. A regular Artur Rubenstein. But there's no music. And I don't think she likes me very much."

Reiko didn't look up. She was hitting the keys with unnecessary force, and muttering deletable expletives under her breath.

Anson hopped down from the desk and thrust a cream-colored envelope in my face.

"Your pay, Mr. Riordan, with the heartfelt thanks of Olin Vanderhof."

I untucked the flap of the envelope and drew out a check on the Farmers' and Ranchers' Bank of San Benito County in the amount of five thousand dollars. We all love checks made out to us in any amount, and I took a moment to admire this one, holding it with thumb and forefinger at the upper right-hand corner. This would more than pay for body work and a paint job on the Mercedes.

Then I slipped the check back into the envelope.

"Anson, old friend, please return this to your employer with my compliments, and tell him I'll claim it when I've earned it. I really didn't find Leonard. He found me. And his being dead doesn't explain anything.

"Tell him also that I am now investigating some shenanigans at his bank, as well as three unexplained murders. Tell him I do this stuff as a hobby. Tell him that Stew Leonard didn't leap off the bridge, he was dead for some time before he was thrown off. And tell him I'd like to see what his accountants have found in the bank's books."

Ward was looking at me with his mouth slightly open and his eyes half-closed. He accepted the envelope without a word, smiled faintly and left the room.

"That is a repulsive little man," said Reiko. She stood, and with a flourish, touched the off-switch of her computer. The display was swallowed in the dark green of the dead screen. "He looks like a lizard and moves like a lizard. He slithered in here and tried to put a lizard move on me, like he was really somebody."

"Hold it, Reiko-san. My impression is that, given a choice, he'd rather sleep with me than you."

"Maybe both, boy. But he's still a lizard. Bet he can catch flies with his tongue." She marched into my office and sat in my big chair, swiveling rapidly from side to side. She pulled out the left bottom drawer (as she had seen me do hundreds of times) and propped her feet on it. "Bet you'd like to know what I've been doing." She looked angry and frustrated.

I tried to look eagerly expectant.

"More wild geese!" she said.

"That's extraordinarily opaque, even for you. What about these waterfowl?"

Then she told me. I once again take the liberty of recreating her adventure:

The idea of Stew Leonard holed up in some rustic cabin in Big Sur had been bothering her. He hadn't seemed the type to repair in solitude to the country. So she did what I had thought of doing. She called the phone company to see if she could get the location of Leonard's hideaway.

"I'm sorry, we cannot give that information." The operator. Funny how those tinny nasal voices you hear exaggerated by comedians are pretty close to the real thing.

"But it's important," Reiko pleaded. "I'm a private investigator working on a case. And I've got to have the information." She thought quickly. "My . . . partner and I are assisting Sergeant Balestreri of the Sheriff's office in this investigation, and . . ."

"Tony?" The voice lost some of its mechanical sound. "God, I haven't seen him for a couple of months. Tell him to call Margie, will you?"

"Sure. And how about that address.?"

"Well, I guess . . . for Tony. Here, let me check the computer. Uh-oh, this isn't going to help you a lot. All it says is Sycamore Canyon Road. Lots o' luck."

"Thank you, thank you. It'll have to do."

Reiko takes the bus to work, and leaves her twelve-year-old Mustang at home. "I will not pay money to park," she says. "I will not feed meters." And she will not accumulate parking tickets the way I do.

When she got the vague location of Stew Leonard's cabin from the telephone operator, she locked up the office and ran to Monterey-Salinas Transit's outdoor depot at the top of Alvarado Street. The bus to Pacific Grove was ten feet out into the street when she banged on the door. The driver, thinking he might have hit something, came to a hissing air-brake stop.

She climbed aboard and dropped her exact change in the hopper. The driver looked at her aghast, shook his head and moved out. Reiko was at her apartment in ten minutes, in the Mustang in another forty-five seconds, and on her way to Big Sur.

She hadn't driven a mile when she got an inspiration. She found a pay phone on Forest Hill and called Greg Farrell.

"Sycamore Canyon Road? Sure, Reiko, I know it. Lots of little places in there...and some big ones."

"Greg, can you help me? I'll be by your place in about twenty minutes. Can you meet me on the road and drive down with me?"

"My pleasure. You still drive that old Mustang? Sorta cad red light? Always liked that color."

"Yep. See you soon."

And off she went in search of Stew Leonard's weekend retreat.

Greg was waiting for her at the roadside. She slowed down but never came to a full stop and he was barely able to get into the car before she zoomed off again in pursuit of *Truth*.

After ten minutes of silence, all Greg could say was, "Do you always drive like this?"

"Sure."

He didn't seem happy with the answer, but he shut up.

Sycamore Canyon Road is just south of the town (one post office, some gas stations, couple of restaurants, and a general store) of Big Sur. It runs west off Highway One out towards the ocean. It is wooded, and the road is narrow and winding.

Reiko drove slowly now, looking for...well, she didn't really know.

Greg understood. "Look for mail boxes, Reiko. Most of 'em have names on 'em."

A half mile after they had turned up the canyon, they found it: a rural mailbox with the flag up. The name on the side, rather sloppily painted, was "Leonard." It stood alongside an opening in the trees that marked the access to a rutted trail back into the woods. Two hundred yards in was the house. A hideaway cabin? From the outside, it was a substantially built two-or three-bedroom house supporting a very tall TV antenna. On the east side and towards the rear of the house was what appeared to be a sheltered hot-tub built for at least eight, and a redwood structure that had to be a sauna. The whole picture was that of a sort of mini-Esalen.

Reiko was moved: "My God, I wonder what Stew Leonard did down here by himself. I really wonder if he *was* by himself. This place looks like it was built for orgies, man."

Greg was thoughtful: "Beats the hell out of my house. But I could never *live* here. Too pretentious."

Farrell is an artist who wishes he could have been a cowboy or a pirate. He wears scrupulously clean faded denim, and a full dark beard. He's enormously gifted and fiercely independent. I've known him a long time, and there hasn't been a minute when I haven't wished *I* were Greg Farrell.

"They got out of the car and approached the house. The front door was locked, of course, and there was a dead-bolt second lock for security. The back door had the same arrangement.

"We're dead," said Reiko.

Greg said nothing. There was a sliding glass door that opened onto the hot-tub-sauna combination. He walked up to it, lifted it easily off its track, and set it aside.

"No sweat," he said.

Reiko pushed aside the drape. They were in what appeared to be the master bedroom.

White. As Leonard's condo was white, so was his not-so-rustic hideaway. Through an open door and a hallway, Reiko could see the living room. Carbon copy is the wrong expression. Carbon paper is black. But everything duplicated the Carmel condo. With one conspicuous difference. This place looked lived in.

The bed was unmade. There were clothes hung on the back of a chair, a litter of junk on the dresser. The bathroom door hung open, and there were towels on the tile floor and half a bar of pink soap on the washstand.

Reiko led the way out into the hall. Straight ahead was the living room, off to the right was another door, probably to a second bathroom.

It was what they call a tastefully appointed small house. Probably furnished by the same tasteful Carmel decorator who did Stew Leonard's condo.

Reiko nosed into every corner, Greg trailing after her, unimpressed by the decor.

"All this guy has got are still life florals and Erte prints. What a jerk!"

When the house had been examined inch by inch, Reiko was exasperated. She had found half a pint of Haagen-Dazs rum-raisin ice cream which she ate just for spite. She had discovered a beautiful negligee hanging in the master bedroom closet.

"Do you think he wore this himself? Na-a-a-ah. He seemed real straight."

Greg, who had politely refrained from asking questions to this point, finally gave in: "*Who* is *he*, Reiko? I helped you break into his house, so I really ought to know, don't you think?"

"He's dead. He was a guy Riordan was trying to find. We found him. Now he's dead. They found him under the Bixby Bridge."

"Oh, *that* guy. I heard about that. Bank manager, wasn't he?"

"Shit, Greg. All this way for nothing."

She sat down on the rumpled bed. On the bedside table was a telephone. A small notepad with a spiral binder lay open alongside the phone. On the exposed page was a phone number. Area code 714, Orange County.

Reiko impulsively snatched up the phone and called the number. She let it ring a while, but there was no answer. Angry, she tore the page out and stuck it in the pocket of her red satin 49er jacket. And promptly forgot it.

She had related all this to me while accompanying her narrative with a gently swaying and rocking of my own beloved desk chair, while I stood, shifting my feet. I've tried to reproduce her tale as accurately as possible, but I may have missed a quote or a preposition or two. She stared in disapproval at a picture I keep on my desk of Imogen Cunningham peering around a tree at a beautiful nude model. She's seen it hundreds of times, but it always call forth that "You're a dirty old man" look.

"Edgar Vanderhof called right after I got back." She was almost *too* casual. "He's got a room at the Monterey Plaza. Says he's made sure his father doesn't know he's in town."

"What did he want?"

"Oh, just asking how we're doing. What do you know and all that." She paused. "*And* he invited me out to dinner."

"And you're going, right? Because he's nice man and tall and good-looking. Reiko, you barely come up to his clavicle. And he's married."

"I know, I know, I know. Don't get excited. I have to eat, don't I? And this guy's probably got *all* the credit cards. Besides, my daddy started me on karate when I was six. I can handle any male up to sumo weight."

I get so goddam possessive about my women. The hot flashes when I saw Sally with Edgar. And now I felt a warmth creeping up the back of my neck. Why didn't the bastard stay in LA? I walked to my window. Reiko swiveled to watch me. Why didn't I take the old man's five thou? Why am I so goddam honest? Nobility is a terrible burden to bear.

I turned to Reiko to say something noble, but she was grinning widely, enjoying my discomfort.

"You're really pissed, aren't you? You're doing your thing with Sally, you had a fling with George Spelvin's wife, and I saw you ogling that career type with the big ass from the bank. How the hell can you get upset over my having dinner with Edgar Vanderhof?"

What's a guy to say? She had me cold. She knows all, sees all, and tell it all to me. I hope *only* to me.

"OK, Reiko-san. Enjoy. But you might do a little something for the firm. See if you can find out anything more about the inner workings of the Vanderhof clan."

"On duty, boss. I'll have him pouring out the family history by nine p.m." She got up and skipped out of my office with a slightly malicious grin on her face.

What I can't figure out is how she found out about my *nuit d'amour* with Debbie Spelvin.

29

"...Edgar's been such a good son. My first born...."

T HE VANDERHOF HOME on Jacks Peak is just what you'd expect it to be: big, old, handsome and impressive. From the road all you can see is a gate with a "No Trespassing" sign on it and a weather-proof phone box to one side from which you may beg for admittance to the grounds. Probably in better days there was a guard here who made the calls after examining the visitors.

I pulled up and made my own call.

Emily Vanderhof answered: "Yes?"

"Mrs. Vanderhof, this is Pat Riordan. I'd like to talk to you and Olin if I may. There are some questions that need answering."

"Olin is resting, Mr. Riordan. Poor man has been so upset these last few weeks. But I'll be glad to help you if I can. Push open the gate when you hear the buzzer."

I followed the lady's instructions. The narrow, tree-lined drive curved uphill and to the right for about two hundred yards, and then opened into a courtyard that looked about as big as the parking lot at Candlestick Park.

I have no idea how many rooms the house contains. The Van-derhofs raised four sons, and each probably had his own bedroom. They had a live-in household staff. They probably had the little amenities, like a billiard room and a music room, God knows what else.

Emily let me in herself. She led me through a dark hall to a small sitting room that was warm and bright and cheerful, in contrast to the somber aspect of the house.

"We can talk here, Mr. Riordan. Olin is sleeping upstairs. Poor dear came home so very tired. I'm worried about him. He's always been so active, even at an age when many men are in retirement homes. But recently...."

"Have you told him Edgar's here?"

"Oh, no. Edgar came at my request, you see. He's the oldest of my sons, and I have always relied on him." I saw tears glisten in the lady's eyes. "I've always prided myself on being self-sufficient, Mr. Riordan. I thought I could weather this storm alone. But Edgar's been such a good son. My first born...."

"You're sure Olin doesn't know he's here? Has no inkling?"

"I'm as sure as I can be. Monterey's not a large city, Mr. Riordan. A lot of people know Edgar, and certainly they would mention to Olin that they'd seen him. One can't control everything."

"Mrs. Vanderhof, has Olin been keeping regular hours recently? I mean, has he been here in the evenings?"

"No, not every evening. And that has bothered me. He's been at his office very late on a number of occasions."

"You're sure of that? You've phoned him there?"

"Oh, no, Mr. Riordan. I never call my husband at the office. We agreed long ago that I could not interfere in business matters." She stared at the oriental rug under our feet. Maybe I should have."

Emily Vanderhof was not the perky, mischievous woman who had been in my office. She looked worn and tired. There were lines in her face I had not noticed before. The sparkle had gone out of her eyes.

"When Olin wakes up, don't tell him I was here. I'll just try to catch him at the office tomorrow. Or soon."

She nodded solemnly, evidently relieved. I drove slowly down the winding road back into Monterey.

I do a lot of serious thinking in the car. That can be dangerous. My mind is sorting out facts while my hands and feet are in control of a self-propelled vehicle going fifty or more miles an hour. Despite this perilous habit, I have never had an accident. I *have* driven past my destination, and often forty or fifty miles out of my way, but never hit anything. Something to be thankful for.

Stewart Leonard was the key figure in this case. But he was dead. He hadn't told me all he knew, and he sure wasn't going to now.

Had I missed something in my investigation of Stewart Leonard? His record was clear. His condo was spotless. If Horatio Alger had written about black people, he would have written about Stewart Leonard. I was a little suspicious of all that off-white furniture, but maybe the guy was just a hell of a housekeeper.

Reiko struck out at the little "getaway cottage" in Big Sur. Her description made it sound more like a sexy partyland for Leonard.

Where's the blue Mercury? Stew left us in Hollister and wound up dead under the Bixby Bridge. The car couldn't have just vanished.

By the time I had searched through all of these thoughts, I was driving through the tunnel to New Monterey, where I didn't really want to be. I made the turn down to Cannery Row because it was there. And since it was evening and I was hungry, I pulled up in front of the little Thai restaurant where I'd met Edgar Vanderhof, just as some thoughtful soul was pulling out with a load of kids who were clutching expensive souvenirs from the Aquarium. I climbed the stairs and found a corner table. The place used to be a French restaurant and it is almost all banquette. The quiet little Thai waitress glided up to me and I ordered a Number 27. I will not embarrass myself trying to pronounce those Thai names. They make it easy by numbering the dishes. I'm partial to 27.

I sat for a quiet while, sipping coffee. There were few customers in the place. I enjoyed my reverie until I heard a very familiar musical laugh coming from across the room. I slid down the banquette a couple of notches and leaned out to see, in a secluded corner of the dining room, my own beloved Reiko, shoulder to shoulder with Edgar Vanderhof, drinking white wine with linked arms.

Flustered, I sprinkled a teaspoon of Thai hot sauce onto my stir fry of chicken, onions, green peppers and cashews, and quickly emptied my plate as tears streamed down my face and my sinuses magically cleared. Then, to avoid a confrontation, I paid my check, overtipped, and sidled out. The little vixen would answer to me in the morning.

30

"That's it. Nice guy, Mr. Heathcote."

I GOT TO THE OFFICE very early the next day. Reiko hadn't arrived yet, which was just fine. I had an itch I wanted scratched, and I wasn't ready to face her.

I called Balestreri.

"Tony, this is not, repeat, not a police matter, but you're a native of these parts and I need some information that I can't get from anyone else. What do you know about a man named Barry Heathcote." I pronounced it "Heeth-coat."

"That's 'Hethkit', Pat. Rhymes with mess kit. He's a sort of shadowy figure. You read a lot about him in the *Herald*. Very prominent in social circles. Gives money to practically every cause. Sort of a recluse. Lives alone down the coast. Alone, that is, with a cook and a houseboy. I handled a burglary down there once. It was easy. We caught the guy trying to hock a piece of carved jade for ten bucks. Guy in the pawnshop had a good eye, and..."

"Whoa, Sergeant. Is this guy old family? How long has he been here?"

"I'm not sure how long. *Not* old Monterey County. Came from back East. Sold some sort of manufacturing business when his wife died, came out here and retired. Ten, fifteen years ago."

I thanked Balestreri for his help. Reiko made some deliberate noises in the outer office.

"Come here a minute, pal, I need your help." I wasn't about to bring up the subject of last night.

I heard her hiss and growl, and I realized that I was tearing her away from her beloved computer. I cannot understand why she spends so much time at that thing. We don't have that much business. Maybe she's doing some accounting on the side.

She appeared, a little angry, a little smug, in the door, and stood tapping the door frame impatiently.

"I've got another name for you to try out on Shiro. Barry Heathcote."

"That's *Hethkit*, dammit. What do you want to know?"

"What do *you* know?"

"Shiro did his landscaping. Talks about him all the time. My uncle, who isn't impressed by people, thinks Barry Heathcote is some kind of nobility. But he still doesn't like *you* very much."

I am aware of Shiro's disapproval of me. He can't be convinced that my intentions towards his niece are honorable.

"I'd like to talk to Shiro. Where can I find him?"

"In his office. Up the hall and around the corner. He's the landlord, remember? Five minutes ago he stuck his head in to say 'hello'."

I found Shiro with his elbows on his desk, his forehead supported by both hands, *absorbing* the front page of the *Wall Street Journal*. He looked up very slowly when I entered his office, and the hint of a scowl appeared on his face.

Shiro Masuda is a wiry little guy, seventyish, whose head of black hair is flecked with gray. Born in Japan, he had come to join his brother in the States after serving in the Imperial Army in WW II. He has a pronounced Japanese accent which I will not attempt to render. There is a certain confusion of l's and r's that cannot be described. When he addresses me, my name comes out something like "Leeldon." That's not really accurate, but it's as close as I can come.

"Shiro, what can you tell me about Barry Heathcote?"

He looked at me without expression, deadpan.

"You mean *Hethkit*. Nice guy, Riordan. What else you want to know?"

"You're a fountain of information, Shiro. You know a lot about everything. As a matter of fact, there's very little going on that you don't know about. Have you seen Heathcote lately?"

"No, Riordan. I landscaped his place down the coast two years ago. He paid his bill promptly. Like some people don't pay their rent on time, y'know. He is a fine gentleman, What else?"

"That's it?"

"That's it. Nice guy, Mr. Heathcote."

He dismissed me with his tone, and glued his eyes back to the Journal. He did not seem to notice when I left.

The only way to conduct an investigation is to ask questions. When you run out of people to question, you go to other sources and ask questions. I went to the library.

I asked questions of the newpaper files. There was much to be scanned. Heathcote had arrived on the Monterey Peninsula just over twelve years ago. Balestreri was pretty close. Heathcote had owned a prosperous electronics firm near Baltimore. When his wife died, he sold out and retired. He took an apartment in Carmel until he found his house down the coast.

Heathcote was active in all the charities, a donor to all the foundations, vigorous in his efforts to protect the sea otter from extinction. He made the society pages of the *Carmel Pine Cone* and the *Herald* regularly. A picture taken at a party showed him beaming at Clint Eastwood. The photograph, taken only months before, showed him to be a portly man of average height, with a full thatch of curly white hair. His right hand held a glass insulated with a paper napkin. His left thumb was tucked in his cummerbund. He looked, I thought, like a "nice guy."

Nothing about him in the business pages, nothing at all. Even the stories about the formation of the Farmers' and Ranchers' Bank didn't mention his name. Everybody else was there: Vanderhof, Caravelli, Fowler, Levine. But no Heathcote.

I was muttering to myself when I left the library. Barry Heathcote was a director of the Farmers' and Ranchers'. I had found nobody on the Peninsula who had seen him or talked to him in the last two months. Even George Spelvin, who claimed to know "ol' Barry as well as anybody", couldn't remember when he'd last seen the man. I resigned myself to another trip down the coast.

It's not that I *really* dread driving Highway One, despite the fact that it's a narrow, two-lane road that has a lot of blind curves and high bridges. But I couldn't find a phone number for Heathcote, and I wasn't going to ask Vanderhof.

When I got back to the office I asked Reiko for a favor.

"What?"

"Would you kindly get your uncle to draw me a simple map of how to get to Heathcote's place. I would be greatly obliged."

"You ninny. Why are you so afraid of a little old man you outweigh by forty pounds?"

"I am not afraid of Shiro, my dear. He just makes me feel uncomfortable. You understand."

"Humph," she said, as she went out the door.

In a few minutes she was back with a precisely drawn map of the Big Sur coast.

"He didn't want to do it, but he did it. See, here's the turn-off. Over here's the house. *Sayonara*, big detective."

The ride didn't seem that long. Shiro's map was easy to follow. The turn-off was well marked, an elegant sign at the roadside reading simply "Heathcote." A well-paved drive wound up the hillside to the house, a sort of imitation Frank Lloyd Wright place that blended into the scenery and followed the contours of the ground.

There were no signs of life around the place. A sharp breeze had sprung up from the ocean. I pulled my jacket collar up and buttoned it.

The house had a double door and a huge knocker, but I used the doorbell. I could hear the chimes inside. No other sound in the house. I pressed the button again. Nothing. Nobody home.

I stood for a few moments on the porch, looking out at the ocean. At the turn-off, Highway One was maybe four hundred feet above the sea. The house was another two or three hundred up the hill. The view was breathtaking. The surf was heavy; the waves crashed against the rocks far below, and sent enormous clouds of spray into the air.

But I hadn't come for the view. I walked down from the porch to the drive. Shiro had done a beautiful landscaping job.

Pure Japanese: simple, understated, elegant. The driveway curved around behind the house. I followed it, thinking that there might be some living soul outside who couldn't have heard the door chimes.

I turned the corner at the back of the house, and stopped short.

Parked in front of a four-car garage was a dirty blue Mercury sedan.

31

"Olin Vanderhof is having an affair."

A<small>N OLD ARMY BUDDY OF MINE</small> used to say, "I did not know whether to shit or wind my watch." Nowadays, when most watches do not wind, the expression means very little. But I had a dilemma. Should I call Vanderhof? Should I report to Balestreri? I did neither. I set a new record for getting back to Monterey.

"Find out anything?" Reiko was looking pretty self-satisfied.

"Uh, yes and no. Talk to you later."

"I saw you last night at the restaurant. You looked like a wild man sneaking out of the place with tears streaming down your face."

I was taken by surprise. "It was the sauce. I got a couple of those seeds and chewed them up. It's something I never do...but I did. Those seeds—they start a little fire inside me. And I cry."

"Were you spying on me, Riordan? If you were, you did a rotten job for a private detective with gray hair and a brilliant assistant. Did you know we were going to be at that restaurant?"

"I had no idea. Pure coincidence. Didn't want to interfere, though. That's why I didn't say hello. Did you have a good time?"

"Lovely time, Riordan. Edgar Vanderhof is one of the nicest men I've ever met. A real sweetheart. Not like some...."

"But his wife doesn't understand him, huh? A marriage on the rocks. They only stay together for the sake of the children. He needs sympathy. He fed you a lot of white wine, took you home, and suggested he stay for breakfast, right?"

"Wrong. He showed me pictures of his wife and kids, took me to a movie, drove me home and shook hands. What do *you* know, person of little faith?"

She had me again. One day, I suppose, when I am in my eighties, I will be able to control this unwarranted possessiveness, this nagging jealously, this soap opera emotionalism. But there is something in my Irish peasant heritage that makes me wildly jealous and over-dramatic. Sally will bring me to earth again. Thank God for Sally.

I stood there feeling that my breath was bad, my armpits stained, my fly open.

"Did you...find out anything?" I asked, meekly.

Reiko folded her arms and leaned back.

"The Vanderhof's marriage has been ideal. They never quarreled in front of the children. They never, *never* raised their voices to each other. They were always together. Or *almost* always together. Edgar noticed a change at a family Christmas gathering. You know how families that are close can sense a change? But he just wrote it off as his mother's arthritis or his father's bad digestion."

She moved around the desk and began a slow version of the little dance step that she uses in time of excitement. Her hands made graceful figures in the air. She had a revelation for me, and she was going to make the most of it.

"Pat, our gentle, kind and aristocratic client has a lady on the side. Edgar doesn't know who. He's sort of flabbergasted. Can't believe his dear old daddy is involved in a romance at his age. But that's what it looks like. Olin Vanderhof is having an affair."

I can honestly say that was the last thing I expected to hear.

"Who's the woman, Reiko-san?"

"They don't know. It's all been very circumspect. Edgar hired a LA private investigator, but he couldn't even get a picture, much less catch 'em *in flagrante delicto*. Papa Vanderhof was always pretty cagey, it seems. The guy got the briefest glimpse of the lady as they were getting into an elevator at the Fairmont in San Francisco."

"Has Emily known about this?"

"As I get it, she has suspected something for some time. But only in the last few months has she allowed herself to believe it. To her, Olin is still the sweet, loving, considerate man she married—when he's with her. But he's been making more and more 'business trips', and staying late more often at the office."

"Why did Edgar tell you all this?"

"'Cause I asked him. You know me, Riordan. I'm not backward. He *had* to tell somebody, Pat. He had kept it from his wife and his brothers. It was boiling inside him. It had to come out."

I tried to get a picture of Olin Vanderhof—tall, thin, mild-mannered, silver-haired Olin Vanderhof—bedding some voluptuous redhead in a hot pillow motel with mirrors on the ceiling. I giggled.

Reiko frowned. "You unfeeling bastard, what's the matter with you? Emily Vanderhof—that beautiful wife and wonderful mother—is being betrayed. And you giggle?"

"Sorry, honey. I just had a vision I can't describe. But I know how you feel. What I cannot understand is why Olin got himself into such a situation. Oh, hell, I *can* understand a man of his years *wanting* to get it on with a good looking young woman. I can even believe in his capability in the sack. After all, some of us last longer than most. But he's so devoted, so loyal, so dignified. . . ."

"So horny! Riordan, you're as bad as he is." She marched indignantly back to her chair and sat, folding her arms and frowning in disapproval of my ambivalent reaction.

What did it mean? Reiko had drawn some startling information out of Edgar. But it had thrown several things out of focus. How reliable was Edgar? I leaned against the frame of the door into my office, and watched as my righteously indignant associate left her chair and arranged herself on that damned uncomfortable Norwegian knee-stool. She punched the power button on her computer, pulled a floppy disk from a small file, and popped it into the machine. In a few seconds lines of tiny bright print appeared, and Reiko's fingers flew around the keyboard, causing changes in the display.

A wild notion hit me.

"Reiko, stop. Listen to me. Can you operate any one of these dinguses? I mean, they all work about the same, don't they?"

She looked up questioningly.

"Sure. If it wasn't programmed in Vietnamese or made in the

Sudan."

"Great! Shut that thing off and grab your coat. We're going to prospect for treasure."

32

"That is the main menu, Riordan."

I DROVE A LITTLE TOO FAST up Munras onto Highway One and over the top of Carmel Hill, down to the Rio Road light where I had to wait for a ridiculously long time to make my left turn. Rio Road to the east runs dead in about three blocks, but ends precisely in front of the condo spread where Stewart Leonard lived. I could only hope the key was still under the mat.

I pulled up in front of Stewart's place and turned to Reiko.

"This, my dear, may be an exercise in futility. Then again, there might be something we can do with Stew Leonard's computer. It is entirely up to you. You know my famous incompatibility with things mechanical. I sent my shaver back to Victor Kiam, my Water-Pik went out of control, and even my electric toothbrush intimidates me. But you, Reiko-san, are in total command of computers. I am depending on you."

She clucked in mild disapproval, and got out of the car. I found the key where I had left it. There was a yellowing *Herald* on the door mat. Somebody apparently had been picking up the mail.

Inside, things were just as I had found them on my first visit. The air was stale and sterile, without the smells of cooking and human presence. I left the door slightly ajar to get some fresh air into the place.

"Holy shit, it looks just like the place in Big Sur. Like the waiting room of a high class whorehouse!" said Reiko, her eyes wide in her

157

appreciation for the white-on-white decor. How she was able to make the comparison I will never know and probably will not ask. Reiko's a mystery I'll never solve. She trotted over and sprawled on a tasteful and expensive couch. "Hey, I could get used to this . . . but in pastels, you know? This is like livin' in a quart of vanilla ice cream."

"We've got business here, Reiko. Upstairs. When we're through, I'll take you over to the Crossroads and buy you a big frozen yogurt with chocolate jimmies."

I led the way up the white-carpeted steps. She bounced along after me, caressing the enameled wrought-iron banister.

The bedroom was dark. Someone had drawn the drapes, I suppose, to keep the sun from bleaching the already white spread and the pale cream carpet. I tugged open the drape on a French door, and the room was flooded with noonday light.

There it was, as I had seen it before, neatly arranged in a corner of the room: Stewart Leonard's computer, in all it's glory, with all its peripheral equipment.

Reiko looked at the set-up with professional admiration. She pulled out a small wheeled chair which had been nested under the computer table, and sat down. Her fingers wandered lovingly over the keyboard.

"It's a good outfit, Riordan. No better than mine—but good."

I am still paying for the electronic equipment Reiko insisted on having at the office. I will probably be paying on it into the next century, if I last that long. There's always some innovative widget to buy.

"OK, little one. Please to begin. I turned it on when I first came up here. I poked around on it but nothing happened."

She looked at me in complete disgust.

"You cannot make a computer function by 'poking around.' You have to have softwear."

The word "software" has always reminded me of toilet paper. I hate computerese almost as much as I hate golf.

"This is your first lesson, Patrick. See this little box? Looks kinda like a small file cabinet? *There's* your software. Let's see what we've got."

She pulled out one of the "floppy disks" (which don't flop) and looked at the label. She opened a slot in another box which appeared to be attached to the main machine and pushed the disk gently in.

Reiko reached around behind the computer and touched a switch, causing the box with the disk in it to hum and some bright dots to appear on the screen. She touched a key. A lot of print appeared.

"That," she said with some satisfaction, "is the menu."

"Order me a little cashew chicken, couple of egg rolls..."

"You're an idiot, Riordan. That is a list of Leonard's personal files. Now we're going to look at 'em."

Her fingers danced on the keyboard. File after file was summoned up, mostly very dull stuff: business letters, memos, a speech for delivery before the Hollister Rotary Club, service presentations for commercial accounts.

We spent an hour and a half going through disk after disk. Nothing but routine stuff. Until....

"Here's something, Riordan. Looks like a series of notes on a bunch of people. Here, let me run 'em through quickly. Then I'll come back and we can start at the top."

They were all there: Vanderhof, Fowler, Caravelli, Levine, Heathcote, four or five others that I'd never heard of, presumably bank directors. Then, key people at the bank, starting with Frances Engel.

Reiko ran the file back up to the top. We began to read Stew Leonard's candid comments on all of his associates at the Farmers' and Ranchers' Bank of San Benmito County. And Stewart was often brutally candid.

Curiously, there was very little on Olin Vanderhof: "Board chairman. Family money. Fairly intelligent. Can be used."

"Can be used." For what? Used by Leonard? Or others?

Eugene Fowler: "Big man from Marin County. Big frame, average brain. Money comes from Marin real estate bought in the fifties, sold in the eighties. A horse's ass, but an honest horse's ass. Wears a bad hairpiece. Wife is pretty much in charge."

Joe Caravelli: "Nice guy. Money from insurance business

inherited from his father, and shrewd play of the market. Quiet, but a good thinker. Good family, nice wife and kids. Honest."

For Harry Levine, something different: "Watch this one. Slippery character. Claims to be an entrepreneur. Can't get a good hold on him. Married but usually away from home. Chases young woman and usually catches them. Asshole. Don't turn your back."

Then the mysterious Barry Heathcote: "Odd duck. Sometimes doesn't seem to know what it's all about. Harmless. I think."

The rest of the board members, some local, some from Monterey County (including George Spelvin), were given bland little notices, and classified as unimportant.

Then came the bank employees, in descending order of importance. And lo, Frances Engel's name led all the rest. Her entry was cryptic: "I know Frances. I know what she can do. Knows how to use her glands. Extreme caution. Brilliant, efficient mantrap."

That was a stopper. In my only encounter with Miss Engel, I observed that she was a generously proportioned woman with a habit of frequently crossing and uncrossing her legs. She hadn't said very much, if anything. But Caravelli and Fowler had considered her important enough to bring along with them.

"Does all this mean anything?" Reiko looked up at me curiously.

"Don't know, kid. Looks like Stew just sat down one day and wrote an evaluation of each of the people around him. Sort of informal. Any way of knowing when he did this?"

She ran the list up and down a couple of times.

"No. He didn't date it. But I'd guess it was early in his time with the bank. What's he mean about the Engel woman. The one with the big..."

"I don't know, Reiko-san. That puzzles me, too. Anything else about her in these files?"

"Didn't see anything. But I'll look again." She ran through disk after disk, at lightning speed, with the skill of one who is passionately devoted to computers.

"Nothing, Riordan. That list was the only interesting thing in the whole schmeer."

Maybe we'd struck out again. Nothing usable in the whole goddam case full of disks. But there was another way to go.

"Reiko, do you know how to use that telephone gimmick?"

Her lip curled in pure scorn as she twisted to look me square in the eyes.

"Is the sky blue? Do birds sing? Is the Pope...."

"OK. Sorry. What does it take to get into the bank's system? From here?"

"*If* the bank's system is on a modem, you have to have a special telephone number and an entry code. You get on the line with the bank's computer. Then you punch the entry code on the phone buttons. Nothing could be simpler."

"OK, do it."

She rose from the chair and pressed her nose against mine.

"You crazy, Riordan? You've ...got ...to ...have ...the ...the numbers. Get it?"

"Well, let's look for 'em."

Reiko was trying to be calm. "Riordan, a guy like Stew Leonard would carry those numbers in his head."

"He could forget. I forget my own phone number sometimes."

"You're *you*. You forget your own name sometimes. He's—was—a bank manager. To them, numbers are their lives." She looked a little dreamy.

"They're also very careful. So let's look around, hey?"

We looked. There was nothing on the computer table except the computer and its wiry tentacles extending to the printer and other paraphernalia. The only paper was the accordion-pleated stuff that fed the printer.

"Nothing, Riordan, nothing. If you want to go downstairs and look through the pots and pans, be my guest. But there's nothing here. Leonard didn't write things down." Reiko tapped the wooden case that held the disks. "He kept everything here."

"What the hell is this?" I held up a little plastic gadget that was connected by a wire to the computer.

"That's a mouse, dummy. It's a thing that makes some computer operations a little easier, 'cause you don't have to use the keyboard."

I turned the thing over in my hand. On the bottom was a small neat sticker on which had been printed a series of tiny numbers and the word "Tuskegee."

"Let me see that," said Reiko, snatching the device out of my hand.

She did a few tricks with the machine and the telephone attachment. Then, very slowly and carefully, she punched out ten numbers on the phone.

On the screen came the legend: "Farmers' and Ranchers' Bank. Confidential file. Enter password."

Reiko's hand trembled as she spelled out the word "Tuskegee." Like the dawn breaking over Yosemite, the machine's screen came alive.

She settled back in her chair, trying to stay calm. She breathed deeply.

"That is the main menu, Riordan. And spare me any more of your goddam Chinese restaurant jokes."

33

"It's easy, Riordan, when you've done it once."

I T TOOK US QUITE A WHILE to get to the right stuff in the bank's computer. But we did get there, and the picture was becoming painfully clear.

Frances Engel's personnel file told us a lot. She and Stew Leonard went back a long way. She had been cashier at the bank branch in Cincinnati, under Leonard. He had brought her out a couple of months after he was hired at the Farmers' and Ranchers'. It was hard to read more than a business relationship into the connection. But who knows?

Frances was the person who assumed Stewart's responsibilities when he was gone. She had a limited power of attorney to sign his name to the documents. She must have known everything that went on in the bank.

Reiko worked feverishly to reach the loan file. When she brought up Sterling Ventures, the deal was all there. Almost. The dates, the amounts, the collateral were all there. The borrower's name was there: Harry M. Levine, CEO. The signatory for the bank: Stewart Leonard, per F.E. The only thing missing was the name that should have followed "Approved by:". What *did* follow was: "See chair."

"Dead end?" Reiko looked up at me and traced the "Approved by:" line with her finger.

I had a queasy feeling in the pit of my stomach.

"I don't know, dear. I don't know. But I've got this bad feeling. Something is trying to dawn on me, and I don't know if I want it to. Let's close up shop and go home."

On the way back, I told her about my visit to the Heathcote place and finding the Mercury.

"Why the hell didn't you call Balestreri?"

"I'm not ready, honey. I can't help thinking this whole Heathcote thing might be a blind alley. And if what I'm thinking is true..."

"What *are* you thinking?"

"I'm not ready, honey. Like I said."

Neither of us said anything more as we drove back over the hill to Monterey. The Christmas decorations were colorful and bright on Alvarado Street, and we rolled into one of those miracle parking spaces that appear to me now and then, as if I were one of the chosen.

I'm sure Reiko wouldn't have guessed the reason for my gloom as we trudged up the stairs to the office. But she held my arm and gave it a little reassuring squeeze.

"I know you're troubled, Riordan. This whole thing has been a bloody mess. Silly. Me and that 'technical advisor' business. I really didn't give a damn about all those silly people or that silly weekend mystery thing. All they wanted to do was drink, anyhow. Some of 'em were belting it in the hotel before dinner. They would have been so hung over the next morning, they couldn't have figured out the clues. I still can't get the one about, 'Behind the soap man's castle on the saddest street in Carmel.'"

"The Gamble estate, honey. The old house faces on Lincoln, but the property runs through to Dolores. 'Dolor', get it? Pain, sadness. Piece of cake."

"Soap?"

"Gamble, Reiko-san. As in Procter and Gamble. At home in Cincinnati. Like Stewart Leonard."

I thought about the magnificent old house and the wooded area around it which, in the last few years, has been "developed" with the construction of new homes. Well, the old money has got to make way for the new money in that single square mile that is

Carmel-by-the-Sea. I remembered a live oak that still grows directly behind the old house. Its dignity is still unsullied, and no builder has had the guts to touch it. Trees are protected in Carmel. You've got to get the City Forester's permission just to prune one. And live oaks are my favorites. They survive, sometimes, a couple of hundred years. But they're susceptible to disease. Strong and proud, nevertheless they die.

"I'm going for a walk," I said abruptly.

Reiko said nothing. She reads me well after all these years. She knelt on her tatami mat and sat on her heels in an attitude of contemplation.

I went into my office and got my blackthorn walking stick.

I left the office without speaking further. Outside, I jay-walked across Alvarado to the passageway that climbs up to Calle Principal. I turned south about half a block to the low adobe building that houses the offices of the Vanderhof Estate.

Anson was not in his customary place in the anteroom. His desk was clear and shining in the subdued light. The scent of his expensive but overpowering cologne was still present. The door to the inner office was slightly ajar.

I walked to it and knocked lightly.

Olin Vanderhof's voice said, "Come in."

I pushed the door open all the way. Vanderhof was seated at a desk even more massive than the one in the outer office. The decor was pure Anson: crossed sabers, coats of arms, more glowering Spaniards. One wall was bookshelves, loaded with leather bound volumes that I suspect had never been opened. The only light source was a polished brass desk lamp.

In the light, Vanderhof looked, as my old Virginia grandma used to say, "like death warmed over." The vertical lines in his long face looked even deeper than they had appeared at our first meeting. The flourescent light of the lamp gave his face a corpse-like pallor, and left his deep-set eyes in shadow. His elbows were on the desk, and he held his fingertips together, as in an attitude of prayer.

"Our business is finished, Mr. Riordan. Oh, I know you returned my check, but I had Anson deposit the money in your bank. Fairly simple thing to do, you know. You've got the money, whether you want it or not. By the way, please close the door behind you. We need no eavesdroppers, do we? People come in and out. And Anson has the afternoon off."

I closed the heavy oak door. Vanderhof indicated a leather-upholstered chair. I sat. From this position, I found that I was looking up at Vanderhof. The old boy plays mind games, I thought. He looked at me gravely, fingertips tapping each other, a slight tic beginning on the left side of his face.

"Mr. Vanderhof, what I originally thought would be the reasonably simple job of finding Stewart Leonard—or, at least, finding out what happened to him—turned into pretty much of a mess. Three people are dead, including Leonard. And it appears that there has been some fraudulent activity at your friendly little country bank. Your own accounting firm has probably informed you of this. It's easy to spot. If I can do it, anybody can do it."

Vanderhof stared at me without moving. I couldn't see his eyes; only the dark hollows.

"I have the accountant's report here before me, Mr. Riordan. It does appear that some six million dollars were paid over to one account in, uh, questionable loans. I'm sure we can get to the bottom of this thing. Our depositors are insured. And it would appear that the men responsible for the, uh, problem are dead."

"Killed, Mr. Vanderhof. Murdered. And it doesn't seem likely that they murdered each other. Levine went first, so he couldn't have killed Shirley Leonard. Stewart had no reason to murder his sister. And some party not yet identified put a bullet into Stewart Leonard's brain and dumped him off the Bixby Bridge. You may think your bank's problem is wrapped up neat and tidy. But there's yet an unidentified perpetrator, as the cops call 'em, who pulled the trigger on three people."

"Riordan, it is up to the police to solve these murders. All that matters to you and me is that you were able to carry out the task for which I hired you, and *you have been paid.* Now, if you'll kindly leave my office, there is business I must attend to."

"I found Leonard's blue Mercury down at Heathcote's place. Know anything about that?"

Vanderhof's head moved slightly, and one hand dropped to his side.

"Nothing, Riordan. Barry's been gone for several months. To a special hospital in Orange County. Altzheimer's. We kept it quiet. I...made the arrangements. I'm his conservator."

There goes the mystery man. I plunged ahead.

"When I got a telephone call that took me to the Carmel River Inn to find the body of Shirley Leonard, I had no idea who the caller was. The voice was hoarse, disguised. It could have been Leonard's voice. Or Gene Fowler's. Or Caravelli's. Or *yours*. At the time, it didn't seem all that important. I figured Shirley could clear that up. But during the last twenty-four hours, I have been able to put together a few things about my client, the respectable Mr. Vanderhof."

He leaned further back into the shadows. The desk lamp was tilted slightly in my direction.

"Olin—I think we know each other pretty well now—much as I dislike the notion, I strongly suspect that you are my man. I suspect that you were romantically involved with Frances Engel. Aw, shit, you were makin' it with her insofar as your capacity would allow. And that in Stew Leonard's absence, with the help of Harry Levine, you siphoned off six million dollars of the bank's funds through loans to a dummy corporation. Why, I don't know. Unless you were buying Miss Engel some pretty goddam fancy presents."

When I stopped, all I could hear was Vanderhof's breathing— slow, deep breaths, as much as ten or twelve seconds apart.

His voice came quietly: "Have you told Emily this? Does she think I've been...unfaithful?"

"I think she suspects, Olin. About some woman, a *femme fatale*. But not necessarily Engel. Or..."

"The murders? The killing of three human beings. The fact that her husband dissipated her inheritance as well as his own in specula-tive oil ventures just before the bottom dropped out in Texas? That he was willing to do *anything* to avoid a family scandal? That he might have created a fool-proof scheme to defraud his own bank and blame it on the bank manager who happened to be a black man? And that to protect himself and his...*honor*, he had to kill three people?"

Vanderhof was in the shadows, and the light was in my eyes. I could hear the tightness in his voice, sense the emotional build-up. I took a two-handed baseball grip on the blackthorn stick.

"It was not really difficult, Riordan. Levine was easy. I entered his hotel room, which was not locked. He was sprawled out asleep, a dead cigar stub in the corner of his mouth. His fat, ugly face was a perfect target.

"Shirley was another matter. I arranged to meet her at the motel. I thought she might know more than she did. At least, I thought she could direct me to Stewart. His absence, as you well know, was a great threat to me. When our interview was over, I stood behind her as she made up her face in a mirror. When she turned, I put a bullet between her eyes. You must have found her as I left her, in a state of quiet repose on the bed.

"As for Stewart. . . . He called me after he left you in Hollister. We arranged to meet at Heathcote's place. He told me that he had pretended not to find the loan file when you went into the bank. Then, after sending you out to your car, he took papers which would. . .incriminate me, and proposed an arrangement that amounted to blackmail. He didn't seem particularly concerned about his sister's death. Only his career seemed to matter. He had spread the papers on a table for me to see. I came round to look over his shoulder. . .and put a bullet in his head."

Vanderhof began to rise slowly from his chair. As his hands reached the desk top level, I could see that his right held a small black automatic fitted with a silencer. I started to stand up, but thought better of it.

"It's easy, Riordan, when you've done it once. Easier still after the second or third time. I think perhaps it would be easier for you if you'd allow me to approach from the rear."

He came out from behind the desk. .

"But I can do it from here. I have always been an excellent shot. I cannot understand what went wrong when I fired at you on the highway. I must have miscalculated the speed of your car."

There was only one move I could make. I dived for the lamp cord, yanked it out, and rolled away from the desk in the pitch blackness. Vanderhof fired at where I'd been, fired again at another spot, twice more toward the back wall when he heard my stick strike the baseboard.

I lashed out wildly with the blackthorn and must have caught him full on the shins. He cried out and fired two more shots at where he thought I was. Each time he fired I saw the small tongue of flame from the silencer in the blackness of the room.

Then suddenly it was quiet. I could hear him breathing, heavily now. I *stopped* breathing and pressed against the wall.

Once more the "sput" of the muffled gun, this time with no flame, and the crump of a body hitting the floor. It was all over.

I felt along the wall for the door. When I opened it, the light from the anteroom fell on the portrait of a stern mustachioed Spaniard on the wall, and the collapsed body of Olin Vanderhof on the floor.

My hand was shaking badly when I picked up the phone to call Balestreri.

34

". . .He should have had nothing to do with Harry Levine and his Sterling Ventures."

An ambulance arrived within minutes. Sergeant Tony Balestreri of the Monterey County Sheriff's Department had taken my call, chewed me out because I wasn't in his jurisdiction, and dialed 911 for the Monterey Police and the medics, something I could have done myself if I had been in my right mind.

As it happened, there was no rush for the ambulance. Vanderhof had done an efficient job, just as he had on the other folks he'd dispatched. A .22 in the ear won't spread a man's brains all over the room, but it's deadly. The ambulance crew did all it could on the spot and rushed Vanderhof to Community Hospital. He was DOA.

Balestreri arrived just after the ambulance left. The Monterey cops on the scene acknowledged his presence with mild annoyance.

He glared at me.

"I am here strictly unofficially, as a friend of the unarmed wonder. How in hell can you blunder into a potentially dangerous situation with nothing but that goddam stick?"

I had recovered somewhat by that time, and responded with some strength: "If I had been Dirty Harry himself, the old man would have had the drop on me. When I came over here I never in this world expected that Vanderhof would try to kill me. If I had, I never would have come. You know me, Tony. I do not place my carcass in jeopardy. But it was just not logical that a respected member of Monterey Peninsula society would pull a gun on me in his own office. I figured he might try to bust my chops—which accounts for the stick—but shoot me? Never!"

"For Christ's sake, Riordan, you suspected that the man had killed three other people. Why should he have a qualm about offing you? You some kind of protected species?"

Balestreri and I have this ongoing argument over handguns. He pretty much subscribes to the "guns don't kill people, *people* kill people" theory. My own position is that the handgun is intended for just one purpose: to put holes in human flesh. And just having one around the house invites its indiscriminate violent use. His view is the lawman's view, and I respect it. My view is that of an ex-foot-soldier who listened to a lot of low-flying lead along the line in Korea, and vowed he'd never touch a gun again.

Neither of us is ever going to win this argument. But we trot it out now and then just to keep in practice.

I answered the questions of the city police and promised to be available when needed. Balestreri took me to his car and drove me back to where I'd left the Mercedes.

"You want me to drive you home, Pat? You look a little shook up."

"Thanks, I'll be all right. I just want to go up to the office and think a while. There are still a few things I want to know about this case."

Reiko had a spread sheet on her computer and was muttering to herself as she tried to balance the office books. She didn't notice me come in right away. When she looked up, her eyes widened, and she said, "Ooooooh."

"What happened to you? Your suit is messed up, your tie looks like it's in your coat sleeve, and you look like you've been rolling around on the floor. You're flushed, and you're holding that stick like you're going to bash me with it." She got up and carefully took the blackthorn out of my hand.

I told her the story. She listened soberly, nodding slightly at intervals. She took my hands gently, led me into my office, and guided me into my chair.

"How 'bout some coffee, Pat? I can run downstairs." We don't keep a coffee maker. Reiko seldom drinks it, and I drink too much when it's available.

"For the first time in a long time, Reiko-san, I feel like a big glass of Dewar's White Label. But coffee will be nice."

She eyed me warily as she glided out of the room. It was Reiko who got me sober when she came into my life, and I know she worries that I might take on a re-match with the bottle some day. But it ain't bloody likely, mate. I've grown too fond of knowing what I'm doing and where I am at all times. And I've come to like myself the way I am. As the saying goes, I was sick and tired of being sick...and tired.

When she returned with a couple of those abominable leaking styrofoam cups of lukewarm black stuff, I had got a pretty good grip on myself. I drained two-thirds of my coffee at first swallow.

Reiko sat on a corner of my desk and arranged herself demurely. She has very nice knees.

"Well, that's that," she said, grimacing as she tasted her coffee. "Things can get back to normal around here."

"You mean boring, Reiko-san."

"Normal, Riordan. Besides, it's the holiday season. Good will and all that."

Not for Emily Vanderhof. In any affair of this kind, there is one who suffers most. This had to be Emily. Her husband of forty-five years had been branded an embezzler, a liar, a philanderer—and a murderer. He had done her a service in taking his own life. There would be no long period of trial by media. The broadcasters and the newspaper people lose interest quickly if a subject is dead. Olin Vanderhof would be buried in the family plot. Despite his Catholic upbringing and his early inclinations to the priesthood, he had become an apostate in his later years, and no monsignor would say blessings over his corpse. Neither would the righteous deny him hallowed ground.

The phone rang.

"*Moshi-moshi*, Riordan's office," said Reiko. She handed the instrument to me. "It's Sally."

"Hello, Frivolous Sal. Long time. What's new?"

"What's new with you, Pat? You haven't called. Don't you like me any more?"

I told her slowly of the events of the preceding couple of hours. For a moment or two there was no sound from her end.

"Oh, Pat. Oh, my God. I simply cannot believe it. Olin dead? Does Emily know yet?"

"I'm sure the Monterey Police have called her by now. Can you get in touch with Edgar?"

"Yeah, I'll call him. I'm going up to the Vanderhofs' house."

"I'll meet you up there, Sally. I'm not very happy about the way this thing ended. I've got a feeling there's more I ought to know."

I hung up and looked at Reiko.

"Could you kinda brush me off and straighten my tie. I'm going to pay a call on a nice lady."

"Stand up, Riordan."

She gave my coat a good brushing. The floor in Vanderhof's office must have been filthy. She brought my errant necktie around to dead center, and tightened the knot. Then she went to the bathroom across the hall to get some wet paper towels with which she carefully swabbed my sweaty face.

"OK, pal, let's go," she said.

"You really want to go with me? You and Sally aren't exactly buddies, you know."

"I'm with you, Riordan. To see this thing through."

We drove out to Jacks Peak. The gate to the Vanderhof place had been left open. When we arrived at the house there were two cars already there. Sally's I recognized. The other was one of those nondescript rentals. Edgar, probably.

I banged the huge brass knocker on the front door. In a moment Edgar Vanderhof opened it. He looked pale and, I thought, nervous.

" Come in, come in," he said, swinging the door wide. I motioned Reiko to precede me, and I trailed along behind. We must have been a ludicrous sight: the small Japanese with a shapeless hat pulled down over her ears, and the wobbly-kneed shanty-Irish detective in a rumpled brown suit and a blue and green muffler against the chill night air, walking down the hushed corridor of the mansion into Emily's small sitting room.

She was sitting on a couch with a handful of tissues pressed to her face. Sally was sitting beside her with an arm around her shoulders, making soothing sounds.

Reiko and I sat in two chairs opposite the couch. Sally signaled with her eyebrows and her mouth that we were to be quiet for a while.

In a few minutes, Emily's sobbing subsided and she became aware of our presence. Sally handed her more tissues, and she dabbed her face with them, scrubbing away in vain at the tear stains.

I had to say something.

"I'm terribly sorry, Mrs. Vanderhof." What a dumb thing to say. But what else? "I certainly didn't suspect...." Maybe I'd better shut up.

Edgar stepped between us.

"I don't think there's anything more for you to say, Mr. Riordan. I really don't know why you're here. My father destroyed himself. Perhaps it was the weakness of age, perhaps naivete, perhaps just foolishness. But he got himself into an impossible situation, and he took the only way out. He should have known better than to enter into a, ah, relationship with the Engel woman. And, God knows, he should have had nothing to do with Harry Levine and his Sterling Ventures. I appreciate your interest. I know your intentions were good. But I think my mother needs to be with the family at this time. I've sent for my brothers and their wives. Sally is an old friend, and she'd better stay, at least until they arrive. Right now, I think you and Miss Masuda had better go."

I could think of no answer to this so I got up, walked to the couch, and patted Emily on the shoulder. Reiko followed with downcast eyes, and mumbled something. I bent down quickly and kissed Sally on the cheek. She squeezed my hand and nodded to Reiko. Edgar stiffly escorted us as we went back down the great hall to the door.

We were heading down the hill on the dark winding road, when Reiko turned to me.

"Wait a minute, Riordan. How did Edgar know about Sterling Ventures?"

35

There were some nasty snags in her pantyhose.

Edgar, the first born, leader of the Vanderhof siblings, the spitting image of his father. He had been in LA for years. He was a successful attorney with a Southern California firm that is drenched with prestige. He had told us that he had responded to his mother's call. His father, he said, didn't know he was in Monterey. He had taken a room in an expensive Cannery Row hotel and was standing by. Standing by for what?

I like to think that my gift of intuition is superior. Which probably means that I'm a good guesser and lucky to have lived to my present age. My intuition had sent me little danger signals when I first met Edgar, and I should have reacted better to them. Instead, I had those hot flashes. I thought the danger was to my relationship with Sally. But it was something more, something I couldn't recognize at the time.

It's not that I suspected Edgar of wrong-doing from our first meeting. He seemed to be just a tall skinny guy who was concerned over his parents' troubles. He was not a creature of forked tongue, nor particularly shifty-eyed. As a matter of fact, he was a harmless-looking, number-juggling type. I might have taken him for a second-string bookkeeper in a very large corporation.

But he knew about Sterling Ventures and the Levine connection. If he had been in town without his father's knowledge, he couldn't have been to the bank. He wouldn't have called his father's accountants. The only logical conclusion was that Edgar had known a lot about the whole situation before he came up from LA on his mother's invitation.

"Well," said Reiko, "what are you dreaming about? I asked you a question and you just stared straight ahead for five minutes. How—and when—did Edgar find out about Sterling Ventures?"

"I don't rightly know, Reiko-san. There's probably a reasonable explanation. Edgar has never seemed like one of the bad guys."

She looked sad. "He was nice to me. I don't want to think he's not what I thought he was. But how do we find out for sure?"

"There's one person who can probably enlighten us. Let's try to give her a call."

By this time we were back on Alvarado Street near the office, but I had to pull around the corner on Bonifacio to park. One of the shortest streets in Monterey, Bonifacio has twenty-minutes meters and a name that map-makers can't squeeze in. I was irritated. My phenomenal luck appeared to have run out. I was going to have to walk half a block.

While I was fumbling with my keys, Reiko turned the knob and the office door opened. We eyed each other accusingly, each blaming the other for extreme carelessness. Until I realized that there was a light in my inner sanctum.

I slipped my blackthorn stick back into the garishly decorated umbrella stand, and pressing my back against the partition, slid along to the open door. Seated in my single guest chair with her very good legs crossed was Frances Engel.

"It was on the radio, Riordan. About an hour ago. Olin killed himself. Confessed to killing Levine and Leonard and the hooker, Leonard's sister. Took a few shots at you, too, I understand. The poor dear man was so terribly depressed."

I looked closely at her face. She had been crying, and her cheeks were flushed and tear-stained. She was kneading and twisting a damp handkerchief in her hands. Her face, which I'd taken to be more than passably pretty when I first saw it, was swollen and sagging. Her tailored suit, which had seemed so right for her on our first meeting, was wrinkled and pulled in the wrong places. Reiko was right. Even when Frances was sitting down, it was apparent that she had a big ass.

But her reaction to the news of Olin's suicide needed some explanation.

"Miss Engel, I think you were, as we used to say, carrying on with Olin Vanderhof. That true?"

Her eyes flashed angrily, but only for an instant. She dabbed at her face with the wet handkerchief.

"He was everything he seemed to be, Riordan. He was sweet, he was kind, he was loyal. Oh, I tried to put the make on him. My position of influence has always been on my back. But he was only paying attention to me because of that rotten bastard, Edgar."

My old vision of Olin making passionate love to some voluptuous creature disappeared.

"I take it you weren't very fond of Edgar."

She uncrossed her knees. For the first time, I noticed her thighs were pretty heavy. There were some nasty snags in her pantyhose. She rested her hands in her lap, threw her head back, and closed her eyes.

"When I first came here at Stew Leonard's invitation, it was great. Stew and I had a little something going in Cincinnati. But that didn't last. He was on a big ambition trip. Had no time for me outside the bank. Then I met Edgar. He came up now and then to see his father. We were thrown together at a party. Edgar's family never came with him except at Christmas or his mother's birthday. So we were two loners hanging onto cocktail glasses on the fringe of a noisy room. He was nice. I was ready. It happened. Whenever Edgar came to Monterey, we'd be together. I could never quite get used to having him show me the latest pictures of his kids before we went to bed, but he was good, he was *really* good."

Reiko was taking all this in from my doorway. I gave her a meaningful look that said, "You got off lucky, kid. Remember the family pictures?"

Frances had put herself into a kind of trance. Her eyes were still closed, and there was a smile on her lips as she dreamed up a fantasy of Edgar being "good." But the expression only lasted a moment. She frowned and went on with her story:

"We had a good thing for a number of years. But then, early this year, Edgar started to cool off. He was having some money trouble. Apparently he had blown most of the money given to him when he left the nest, and was trying to find a way to raise more. I'm not sure what he was doing. But he kept pumping me about the bank. I told him I couldn't help him, but I thought I knew who could. I introduced him to Harry Levine."

Her eyes were open now, staring straight ahead at a day-at-a-time calendar on my wall that was a little over three weeks behind.

"Harry had always represented himself as a big money man from San Francisco. I thought he might put Edgar in touch with the sources he needed. Edgar was always terrified that his father would find out about his problems. The Sterling Ventures set-up was Harry's idea. Edgar would be his partner. They would milk the bank for as much as they could, fasten the blame on Stew Leonard, and split the take. Edgar still had me in his pocket, so I went along. I could handle the mechanics of the deal when Stew went on vacation."

She sat bolt upright and turned to me.

"Olin found out. I don't know how. He had always seemed oblivious to the day-to-day workings of the bank. Edgar told me later that the old man had confronted him in a rage. It must have been too much for him. To protect his wife and his family, he set about to cover for his rotten, stinking son. Oh, I'm sure he killed them, Levine and the Leonards. I even think he meant to get caught. Maybe that's why he hired you. Then he changed his mind and tried to pay you off. Oh, Jesus, Riordan, that sweet old man was never meant to be a killer."

She began to sob convulsively. Reiko moved to her side and put a hand on her shoulder.

I sat in my chair and looked across the desk at Frances Engel. She's guilty of some kind of conspiracy to defraud in San Benito County, I thought. She just confessed to me. But no way is she subject to a homicide indictment. However, I didn't want Olin to have all the blame laid on him. What I had to do was get Edgar, and get him good.

36

"We represent law and order, and we've got to see Edgar Vanderhof now."

I CALLED THE VANDERHOF HOUSE. Sally answered.

"Sal, is Edgar still there? There's a small matter I'd like to talk to him about."

"He left, Riordan. He took one of his father's cars and said he was going back to his hotel to pick up his things. He's going to stay here for a while."

"What kind of car?"

"The Ferrari, I think. He always coveted it. Funny, that was Olin's baby. He'd always wanted one and only got it four or five years ago. Never drove it fast. Just liked the feel of it."

"What color?"

"What else? Fire engine red. Hey, that's an old expression, isn't it? Fire engines are white or yellow now, aren't they?"

"Some are. How long has Edgar been gone, Sally?"

"Oh, gee, maybe ten minutes."

"Thanks, sweetie. I'll be talking to you."

I turned to Reiko: "Get your hat. We're going for a ride."

"I've got my hat on, dummy. Where are we going?"

"Plaza Hotel. To catch up with Edgar."

Frances Engel had been sitting quietly, sniffing into her soaked handkerchief. I grabbed a box of tissues off my desk and dumped it in her lap. "Enjoy," I said.

I ran out of the office with Reiko at my heels. I don't usually move that fast, and I cannot explain why I did not plunge headlong down the stairs and fracture my skull.

We raced around the corner and got into my car.

I muttered a short prayer to the effect that the Monterey Police should be elsewhere, and took off across Bonifacio to Washington and swung left towards the Bay. With some luck on the lights, I was in the Lighthouse tunnel in a couple of minutes. Reiko didn't say a word, but she sat, tight-lipped and wide-eyed, strapped in and clutching at the dashboard.

I took the Cannery Row turn-off and in another minute came in sight of the Plaza Hotel. Parked in the white curb zone in front of the hotel was the red Ferrari. I pulled up behind with a heroic screech of the tires.

We dashed into the lobby. A gray-haired desk clerk with a bristling guardsman's moustache looked startled as I banged my stick on his counter.

"Edgar Vanderhof, please. Which room?"

The clerk raised his eyebrows.

"I'm sorry, sir, I can't give you that information. However, you may call from the house phone, just over there. Ask for your party by name. You'll be connected."

The man had one of those phony London West End accents and I was desperate. I didn't want Edgar to know I was coming. I feigned indignation.

"That is bullshit, my friend." I whipped out my wallet and gave him a flash of a card which reads, "Honorary Sheriff of Monterey County, 1985–86." "We represent law and order, and we've got to see Vanderhof *now*."

He looked at Reiko in total disbelief, but he said, "308. Take the elevator." And he turned his back.

Edgar's door was open when we arrived. He was carefully packing, as a good lawyer would, placing things in a suitcase just so. A large garment bag lay across the bed. He didn't hear us enter.

"Hi, Edgar. Understand you're movin' to the big house. Fixin' to sell it, maybe? Ought to bring a pretty good price. It's a wonder General Sherman left it standin' ain't it?"

It is hard to describe the look on Edgar's face. There was astonishment, fear, and what looked like gas pain.

"What are you doing here, Riordan?"

"Just had a little talk with Miss Frances, Edgar. Little lady told us
some pretty interesting things about you. And Harry Levine. *And*
Sterling Ventures. She also said you and she had had a few waltzes.
Real good friends you were, she said."

"The woman's a vicious liar and an opportunist. She tried to get
my father—my seventy-year-old father—into bed. Anything she
may have told you is a rotten lie."

"I don't think so, Edgar. Besides, you told my little friend here
that Olin was having an affair, didn't you? And, as a matter of fact, I
think everything Frances told us is the truth. I think *you're* the liar,
Edgar."

He seemed to gain better control of himself.

"Look here, Riordan, this thing can all be cleared up. I'm checking out of here and going up to my mother's. You and Reiko can
follow me up the hill and we'll talk it all out."

That seemed reasonable enough at the moment. Edgar snapped
shut his suitcase, slung the garment bag over his shoulder, and
started out of the room.

"All right, Edgar. I'd like to hear you tell your story in your
mother's presence. Let's go."

He had already taken care of the bill, so we marched right across
the lobby and out the door to his car. Reiko trailed along behind,
holding the other end of my blackthorn stick.

I helped him stow his baggage in the Ferrari.

"See you on the hill, Riordan." He smiled and waved as he got in
the car. The Ferrari's engines throbbed, and Edgar roared away in a
cloud of dust.

Reiko screamed: "He's not going home, Riordan! The bastard is
taking off!"

A goddam car chase? I felt a wave of panic. Hell, that's what they
do in TV shows when the writers run out of ideas. But I had no stunt
guys to call on.

"Oh, God, Reiko. I can't catch him. The Mercedes needs a
tune-up, and the tires are no damn good."

"I'll drive!" she yelled, knocking me out of the way with a shoulder to the solar plexus. And soon we were rocketing along after the Ferrari while I tried clumsily to fasten my seat belt.

I will never forget that ride. We were lucky to catch sight of Edgar. He hadn't reckoned with the Cannery Row traffic, and we got within a hundred yards of him at the American Tin Cannery. He was taking what he remembered to be the least congested route around the Peninsula, probably heading for Highway One. It's a great ride for the scenery, but I wasn't watching the scenery.

The Ferrari slithered in and out of traffic and Reiko followed suit. She was grim at the wheel, her hat pulled down to her eyebrows, hands clamped on the wheel at the 10 and 2 positions, foot heavy on the accelerator. My brake foot kept stabbing the floor boards instinctively.

Up Forest Hill we went, keeping the Ferrari just in sight. I remember thinking that at least we were near the hospital up there and had a fair chance of surviving. We passed the hospital at great speed, and plunged down the hill to the Highway One on-ramp. It was just beyond here that I'd been shot at by Olin Vanderhof.

As we hit the highway, we saw some congestion up ahead. Cars were stacked up at the Carpenter Street traffic light. The Ferrari got over on the shoulder, and we followed it down Carpenter into Carmel.

"Here's where we get it," I thought. The streets of Carmel, ol' Clint's town, are narrow and dark, and many of 'em innocent of traffic signs. It is the holiday seaon, and there will be thousands of automobiles and tour busses on the streets.

The red Ferrari barely slacked its speed. Reiko matched every turn, and even though we couldn't close the gap, we kept the Ferrari in sight.

We were on Junipero, a wide street, divided by two rows of parking spaces. Miraculously, the traffic seemed to part for Edgar like the Red Sea for Moses, and we snuck in behind. I wondered where the Carmel Police were, and guessed that the entire force had been drawn to a block south of Ocean to handle a complaint about a barking dog.

Junipero is like a roller coaster, and joins Rio Road at a blind intersection that Edgar went through at fifty miles an hour. Reiko whipped through after him, narrowly missing a station wagon full of nuns from British Columbia.

We went past the Mission at sixty, Edgar still out ahead by a hundred and fifty yards. He slowed down only slightly as he turned right into Oliver Road.

"Oh, my God," yelled Reiko, "he doesn't know!"

Oliver Road used to be a short cut from Rio Road to the highway until the nice residential folks in Mission Fields got together and had it blocked to get rid of the noise of the drag racers. Now there is a cable fence flanked by huge boulders at the highway end.

The sound of the crash came in seconds. Edgar, having been out of the area except for occasional brief visits, had not known about the barrier. When we reached the scene, it was all over.

Spotting the barrier too late, he had tried to cut left, and the speeding car couldn't respond. It skidded sideways into the barrier and rolled, coming to rest in front of the office of the Carmel River Inn, the place where I'd found Shirley Leonard's body.

Contrary to the impression you might have from watching innumerable television crime shows, cars do not always burst into flames when they roll over. The Ferrari was overturned, the wheels still spinning. It had rolled at least three times, and the top was flattened against the body of the car. I ran to it, but there was no sound, not much hope. The doors were hopelessly smashed shut. I wondered, rather stupidly, if Edgar had fastened his seat belt. There wasn't much of him to be seen in the wreckage.

Somebody called the fire department, the sheriff, and the ambulance. Reiko and I went back and sat in the Mercedes, holding hands.

She brought a crumpled piece of paper out of her jacket pocket. "It's a phone number, Riordan. Orange County. Got to be Edgar's. Found it in Big Sur."

I nodded. "Hey, small one, when I was driving down to the hotel, you were scared to death. How could you handle a chase like that?"

"I'm only nervous when *you* drive, Riordan. Your reflexes, you know. After all, you're . . . . " She thought better of it, and shut up.

37

"He was my idea of an everlasting live oak...."

A FEW DAYS LATER, Sally and I were taking one of those long Carmel walks on a picture-book Carmel December day. She doesn't object to the Peninsula in December. December is *supposed* to be cold. We had arisen early, had breakfast at the Little Swiss Cafe, where they make their own croissants and the best blintzes in the West. Then, feeling well-fed and relaxed, we headed south on Dolores.

You've got to choose your Carmel walks according to how you feel. If you walk downhill, you have to come back uphill. Now that's a profound observation, isn't it? If you begin your walk uphill, you can coast back. South on almost any street is downhill.

"Did I tell you that Emily is going down to live with her second son in La Jolla? With Olin gone and Edgar gone, she's selling the place on Jacks Peak. She's a strong woman, Pat. She'll recover. She'll never get over losing her husband and her eldest in such a bizarre way—but she's strong."

We walked on half a block or so.

"It's funny," I said, "how you size up people. I'm supposed to be able to do that. I may be the world's most untalented private investigator. But I could have sworn that Olin Vanderhof was incapable of murder. When he came into my office the first time, he seemed so damn nice, so quiet, even shy. How can a guy like that do what he did?"

"There was a lot of pride there, Patrick. A lot of love. I think that in Olin's mind he was a sort of vengeful white knight, protecting his own at all costs. The people he killed—so efficiently—were without much value in his scheme of things, compared to those he loved. I think he might have had some respect for Stewart Leonard—until Leonard came at him with a blackmail proposition."

We were down past Twelfth Avenue by this time, and the slope began to get steeper.

"Edgar had 'em fooled, I guess. Had you fooled, Sal, even though you'd known him so long. Honest, now, it is true that he never tried to sneak a feel, never accidentally grabbed your chest?"

"You are impossible, Riordan. Edgar never laid a glove on me. Not that I wouldn't have enjoyed it."

Between Thirteenth and Santa Lucia, I stopped.

"'Behind the soap man's castle on the saddest street in Carmel,'" I said.

"What the hell are you talking about?"

"This is the place. And what I said to you was a clue in that crazy 'mystery weekend' that Reiko was involved in. They were going to have the dues-paying gumshoes find something here to solve the mystery of the slaying of Rhett Carstairs."

"Who?"

"Believe it. See—through those trees. That's the old Gamble mansion. All this property was part of the estate before they cut it into lots. And we're behind it."

Sally put her hands on her hips. "So who gives a damn?"

I walked off the street onto a dirt driveway that led to a decaying garage. To the left was one of my favorite live oak trees, a classic old tree with twisted limbs that reached out and up in every direction.

"It's still here, Sal. I'll always think of Olin Vanderhof when I see this tree. He was my idea of an everlasting live oak, living with the storms, bending but not breaking. But I guess he was mortal, and this good old tree is mortal, too.'"

Sally was looking at me in wonder.

"Why, you philosophizing, sentimental sonofabitch. Kiss me!"

And to the dismay of two elderly ladies slowly climbing the hill, Sally and I locked in a passionate embrace.

About the Author

Roy Gilligan has been a radio-TV personality, a newspaper columnist, and a teacher. He has written for the *San Francisco Chronicle, San Jose Mercury-News, Monterey Herald, San Francisco Focus,* and Whodunnit Productions, among many others. Mr. Gilligan lives in San Jose, California, with his wife of 41 years. He has one daughter and fond memories of four of the nicest dogs that ever lived.

If you enjoyed LIVE OAKS ALSO DIE, there's a chance that you might like CHINESE RESTAURANTS NEVER SERVE BREAKFAST, the first book in this series.

You may order additional copies of LIVE OAKS ALSO DIE, or its predecessor CHINESE RESTAURANTS NEVER SERVE BREAKFAST. Just send $8.95, check or money order, plus $1.50 postage and handling, to:

Brendan Books
P.O. Box 710083
San Jose, CA 95171-0083

(California residents add appropriate sales tax)

These books are also available through local bookstores that use R. R. Bowker Company BOOKS IN PRINT catalog system. Bookstore discount available through publisher.

What critics said about CHINESE RESTAURANTS NEVER SERVE BREAKFAST:

". . .Gilligan creates a new Island of diverting mystery. He hits the notable nail of Carmel squarely on its quaint little head with a highly competent romp."
—Gus Arriola, creator of *Gordo* and long-time Carmel resident.

"Gilligan's sleuth is likable, his characters (from trendy Carmelites to moneyed Pebble Beachers) ring true to type, and the author writes with an assured sense of the irony between Carmel's charming ambience and troubled residents."
—Howard Lachtman, *The Stockton Record.*

"It's hard to tell which is more enjoyable in Roy Gilligan's first— and hopefully not last—mystery novel: a fast-paced whodunit murder plot or the detailed and skillful depiction of the Monterey Peninsula."
—Kevin Howe, *The Herald,* Monterey, CA.

"Gilligan has managed to cook up a book that is more nourishing than fast food. Readers can hope he stays in the kitchen."
—Liz Ciancone, Terre Haute, IN, *Tribune-Star.*